Cruisin

Cruise Ship Christian Cozy Mysteries Series
Book 9

Hope Callaghan
hopecallaghan.com
*** *** ***

Copyright © 2017
All rights reserved.

Visit my website for new releases and special offers:
hopecallaghan.com

Thank you, Peggy H., Jean P., Cindi G., Wanda D. and Barbara W. for taking the time to preview *Cruisin' for a Bruisin',* for the extra sets of eyes and for catching all my mistakes.

A special thanks to my reader review team: Alice, Amary, Barbara, Becky, Becky B, Brinda, Cassie, Christina, Debbie, Denota, Devan, Francine, Grace, Jan, Jo-Ann, Joeline, Joyce, Jean K., Jean M., Kathy, Lynne, Megan, Melda, Kat, Linda, Lynne, Pat, Patsy, Paula, Renate, Rita, Rita P, Shelba, Tamara and Vicki.

i

TABLE OF CONTENTS

Chapter 1

Millie Sanders watched as her boss, Andy Walker, Cruise Director of *Siren of the Seas* cruise ship cleared his throat and approached the makeshift podium. All available ship's crew had been called below deck to attend a last minute meeting, which had never happened before.

Rumors had been swirling around the ship for weeks that there was going to be a change in schedule. She'd heard they were having engine problems, that the ship's booking schedule had dropped off dramatically and they were going to reposition the ship to a European port to attract more passengers.

The final rumor she'd heard was that a larger cruise line – a competitor, was buying out Majestic Cruise Lines and all positions on board the ships would have to be renegotiated.

Millie glanced at the large diamond solitaire ring Nic - Captain Armati - had given her a month ago when he proposed on a small and secluded Caribbean island.

Millie had hinted around to Nic she'd heard the rumors but the only thing he told her was that she needn't worry.

She didn't pressure him to tell her. Millie, Siren of the Seas' Assistant Cruise Director, was treated like any other employee on board the ship, with the tiny exception of her future husband.

Donovan Sweeney, the ship's purser, stood next to Andy. The men exchanged a quick glance before Andy shuffled forward.

"Attention everyone." Andy spoke into a microphone but it wasn't necessary. His voice was loud and booming. Even the crewmembers who couldn't fit inside the large room and stood out in the outer hall grew silent.

"We've been asked to meet with all of you today to dispel some rumors flying around the ship and to let you know when the ship docks this Saturday; we won't be bringing on any new passengers."

An echo of gasps filled the packed room.

Andy held up his hand. "Majestic Cruise Lines has not been sold, merged or filed bankruptcy. Our ship, Siren of the Seas, has been chosen for dry dock improvements. We will be in our home port of Miami for one week while workers install new guest activities on the upper decks. We also plan to renovate *Waves* to improve traffic flow and spruce it up."

Waves, the ship's buffet, was one of the busiest areas on board. During peak hours, it was nearly impossible to move around and the lines of passengers waiting for food were long. "If the dry dock project is successful, Majestic plans to roll the program out to the other ships in the fleet."

One of the crewmembers raised his hand.

"Yes." Andy pointed at him.

"What happens to the crew? Will we stay on board the ship?"

Andy explained all crew would remain on board to help with the deep cleaning of all areas. Housekeeping would deep clean cabins, kitchen staff would deep clean eating areas as well as the galley, and maintenance would be responsible for painting, polishing and making minor repairs where needed.

Annette, Millie's close friend and the ship's director of food and beverage, nudged her. "A week parked in Miami will give us time to shop for your wedding dress."

Millie was still processing the fact they were going to be sitting in the homeport for an entire week. It would be the perfect opportunity to squeeze in some wedding shopping. "Yeah. Sounds great."

Andy finished by explaining all crew work schedules for the various departments would be posted the next morning.

Millie waited for the room to clear before she wandered to the front where her boss stood chatting with Donovan and Felix, one of the ship's dancers.

"...which will be a great time to work on the new show *Waves of Wonder*," Andy told Felix. After Felix left, Millie stepped close. "So this was the big news."

Andy grinned. "I know you've been chomping at the bit to know what was going on but we just got the final word this morning it's a go – I mean – stay. I knew something was up last month when I went over the upcoming passenger roster and noticed no one was cruising next week."

"So what passenger enhancements are being added?" Millie asked.

"Workers will install a rock-climbing wall adjacent to the mini golf course and cantilevered hot tubs with see-through floors on both sides of the ship, one deck above the main pool."

Millie narrowed her eyes as she thought about the new additions. "The workers will be able to get all that done, including cleaning and renovating *Waves,* in a week?"

"It's an ambitious plan," Donovan said. "That's why we're the guinea pigs, to see if we can actually pull it off."

"And if we can't?"

"Failure is not an option," Andy said. "Siren of the Seas is sold out for the following week and we're already advertising the ship's new features."

Donovan slapped Andy on the back. "Thanks for handling the announcement. I need to get back upstairs."

After Donovan exited the dining room, Andy motioned her to follow him into the hall. "We will have shifts of crewmembers working 'round the clock to get the job done, which means Dave Patterson and his men, along with some outside security personnel, will be working 'round the clock, too."

"To keep an eye on the temporary workers?" Millie asked.

"Yes. We'll have a lot of new faces around the dock area and in many areas of the ship."

Millie's mind raced as she wondered what she would be doing – her...their job was to entertain guests and if there were no guests, there was no work.

They slowly strolled down the ship's main corridor, nicknamed I-95 for its size and length. It ran from stern to bow and was the crew's main travel path. It connected crew quarters to crew common areas like the dining room, crew laundry area and even the lounge area where crewmembers hung out during their precious free time.

Andy glanced at his watch. "I'm on my way to the theater to chat with the rest of the entertainment staff who weren't able to make it to the meeting.

I want to head off the rumors before they get out of hand."

Millie and Andy parted ways at the stairwell. It was time for Millie to host the Mix and Mingle singles afternoon painting party, which she'd never done before. Mainly because of Danielle, Millie's cabin mate, who also happened to be part of the entertainment staff and typically hosted the event.

The painting party was Danielle's favorite activity. She'd brought home all of her works of art, ranging from floral arrangements to mountain scenes. The artwork filled Danielle's entire bunk area and started to creep down the wall toward Millie's bunk. Her most recent masterpiece was a painting of Siren of the Seas.

Danielle had recently come down with a bad cold and Millie offered to cover her shift so she could rest.

The remainder of the day was a blur as Millie hustled from one end of the ship to the other to host the scheduled events.

Thankfully, Danielle was feeling better by later that evening and insisted she could pick up her shift the following day. Millie relayed the information on the upcoming dry dock.

"I bet Andy is going to make us work our tails off. This is gonna be the worst week of my life," Danielle moaned.

"It won't be that bad," Millie said. "Besides, why does it matter what we do?"

The next couple of days flew by and the ship's crew began preparing for the upcoming week. It was so hectic; Millie only had time to squeeze in a quick visit to Captain Armati, who also seemed preoccupied with the upcoming week in port.

A nagging sense of uneasiness had settled over Millie and she chalked it up to the change in schedule.

By the time Millie felt the familiar shudder of the ship as it docked in Miami early Saturday morning, her uneasy feeling had turned into a deep sense of foreboding.

She hadn't been able to sleep a wink so she crawled out of bed, dressed for the day and made her way to an upper deck to admire the lights of the city as they drew close to their home port.

The massive cruise ship inched its way into the channel. Off in the distance Millie could see flashing lights. As they drew closer, she noticed one of them was an ambulance and the other a police car. They were parked in front of the dock where Siren of the Seas berthed.

A chill ran up Millie's spine. They were waiting for Siren of the Seas to dock.

Chapter 2

Millie leaned over the railing and glanced in the direction of the bridge house and the section that extended over the side. She caught a glimpse of several shadowy figures standing inside the bridge and was certain one of them was Captain Armati.

The water whirled in fast swirls as the ship began to shudder and ease into the open spot. Millie watched the ship's crew throw the mooring lines to the men waiting on the dock. The men dragged the thick ropes to the bollards and secured the lines.

After the ship was secure, two workers rolled the ramp into place and the ship's gangway door opened.

Two police officers climbed out of the patrol car, joined the ambulance driver and EMT who were standing next to a stretcher and approached the ramp.

"Whatcha' looking at?"

Millie gasped as she spun around, clutching her chest. Cat, Millie's friend, stood behind her. "You scared me half to death."

"Sorry. I couldn't sleep." Cat shivered. "I'm all wound up about us being in port for a week."

"Are you worried about Jay?"

Jay Beck was Cat's ex-husband. He was in prison for attempted murder - Cat's attempted murder - not once but twice.

He'd escaped from prison not long ago and tracked Siren of the Seas to a remote island where he kidnapped his ex-wife and tried to finish what he'd started years earlier.

It had taken Cat several months of counseling to deal with the trauma of the incident and she was just getting to the point where she was comfortable enough to leave the safety of the cruise ship.

"Yeah. I feel vulnerable sitting in port." She eyed the dock nervously. "Maybe I'll just hang out here for the week. There's no reason for me to go into the city."

"I was thinking of shopping for my wedding dress," Millie said. "Won't you at least come out for an afternoon with Annette and me?"

Cat bit the edge of her lip. "I...we'll have to see." She quickly changed the subject. "What's going on down there? I've never seen a cop car or ambulance waiting for the ship; of course I'm usually still in bed when we dock."

"Yeah. Same here." Millie shifted her gaze.

The ambulance driver and EMT pushed the stretcher up the ramp while the officers followed behind and they disappeared inside the ship.

It wasn't unheard of for an unruly, usually inebriated, passenger to get into a brawl during a cruise. If the incident were severe enough, security would place the passenger or passengers in the ship's holding cell until they reached port.

"Maybe it's a passenger they're pulling from the hoosegow," Millie said. "Or someone got hurt during a fight in one of the bars."

A short time later, the ambulance driver and EMT wheeled the stretcher down the ramp. There was someone on the stretcher.

Millie squinted her eyes. "Is that Brody?" 'Brody' was Brody Rourke. He had recently been promoted to head of night security on board the ship.

"Yeah. I think it is. My money is on an unruly passenger who had a few too many and ended up attacking Brody when he tried to break up a fight," Cat said.

Dave Patterson, head of security, along with the police officers, followed Brody and the medical personnel onto the dock.

"Patterson must be filing a report," Millie said. She could see one of the officers jotting notes in a notepad as he talked to Patterson. After several moments, the officers climbed into the police car, turned the overhead lights off and sped away.

The ambulance...and Brody, had already left.

"Maybe there's more to this than meets the eye," Millie said as she shifted her gaze to the skyline and the morning sun creeping over the horizon.

"Millie, do you copy?"

Millie plucked her radio from her belt. "Go ahead Andy. I'm here."

"I'd like to see you in my office as soon as possible."

"10-4. I'm on my way." Millie clipped her radio to her belt. "Andy and an early morning meeting are never good signs."

"Good luck," Cat said. "I need to head back to my cabin and get dressed."

Millie took a closer look at her friend and a slow smile spread across her face. Cat was sporting pink plastic rollers in her hair, a paint spattered pair of jogging shorts and neon pink t-shirt which matched the hair rollers. Emblazoned on the front were the words *Stay Calm and Cruise On*. "I love your shirt."

Cat tugged on the bottom. "Catchy huh? We just got these in. We have them in neon blue, purple, pink, yellow and green."

The women began walking toward the side stairs. "I'm in charge of revamping *Ocean Treasures*. I've been meaning to do it for a while but never had enough time."

Ocean Treasures was the ship's gift shop. "Would it be because all of your free time is spent hanging out with the hot Doctor Gundervan?" Millie teased.

Cat punched her friend in the arm. "Of course not."

"Cat."

"Okay. Yes. Joe and I spend more time together than we probably should. I keep telling myself we need to cool our jets and take it slow but instead of slow, I feel like we're moving fast forward."

Millie didn't know the ship's doctor very well. Her only concern was Cat not get hurt in a shipboard romance, although Millie had no room to talk. That's exactly what she'd done with Nic, but hers was headed toward a happy ending...the altar, at least she hoped it was.

Corporate frowned on shipboard romances. Marriage between an officer and ship staff or crewmember was unheard of. In other words, unless Nic and Millie could figure out a way around their dilemma, Millie would have to quit her job or transfer to another ship. They could not live onboard the ship, both remain working and live their 'happily ever after'.

The women parted ways in the stairwell as Cat continued toward the crew quarters and Millie walked to Andy's office, located behind the theater. She caught a glimpse of a faint glow peeking out from the bottom of Andy's office door.

Millie knocked softly before opening the door and stepping inside. Her boss was seated at the head of the small conference table in his usual spot, but instead of hunched over his infamous "black schedule book," he was staring blankly into space.

"Millie." He snapped to attention.

"I'm sorry. I knocked. I didn't mean to scare you."

"It's okay. I was just a little distracted." Andy patted the seat next to him. "Have a seat. Danielle is on her way down."

"You woke her up?" Millie asked. "Great. She's going to be cranky the rest of the day."

"Who's cranky?" Danielle ambled into the office.

"Nice do." Millie grinned as she pointed at Danielle's blonde hair, matted on one side and sticking up on the other.

"What?" Danielle raked her fingers through her long locks. "Andy said he needed me down here ASAP." She eyed Millie's uniform and meticulously groomed hairdo. "Did you sleep in your clothes?"

"No. You were out like a light. I woke early and got ready before heading upstairs to watch the ship pull into port," Millie said. "The Miami skyline in the early morning light is gorgeous. I even caught a glimpse of the beautiful mansions on Palm Island all lit up."

"Meh." Danielle yawned. "You won't catch me up that early. Maybe someday but don't hold your breath. I like my sleep too much." She turned to Andy. "So what's the 411?"

Millie turned her attention to Andy.

"I want to go over a couple things before passengers start disembarking this morning. We had a brief meeting with Donovan Sweeney late last night to go over the schedule."

Donovan Sweeney, Siren of the Seas' purser, was also in charge of both the ship's crew and staff.

Danielle leaned forward. "Let me guess. You're giving Millie and me a week off paid since we won't have passengers on board."

"Not even close. You'll still be responsible for helping get the ship shipshape." Andy chuckled. "Get it? Shipshape."

Danielle rolled her eyes.

"Here's your detailed list of duties for the coming week." Andy slid a sheet of paper toward Danielle and another toward Millie.

Millie slipped her reading glasses on and scanned the list. "Clean, organize and help repair stage costumes, inventory, update and replace trivia materials, update the karaoke playlist." She set the paper down. "Looks good to me."

"What?" Danielle gasped as she studied her list. "Inventory library books, check board games to make sure all the game pieces are there." Her eyes widened. Millie couldn't wait to find out what was next on her co-worker's list. "*Clean the bingo balls?*" She waved the sheet of paper in Andy's face. "How do you clean bingo balls?"

"Thanks for the reminder." He motioned for Danielle to hand him her sheet and he quickly scribbled a side note and handed it back. "You need to weigh them too, to make sure all bingo balls are exactly the same."

For once, Danielle was stunned into silence. All Millie could think of to say was, "Danielle's least favorite place on board the ship is the library."

Danielle crumpled the paper and began forming a ball. Andy cleared his throat and she uncrumpled the paper. "Okay but I object."

"On what grounds?" The corners of Andy's eyes crinkled as he fought to keep from laughing.

"Inhumane treatment of an employee."

"I'll trade your least favorite to-do item for one of mine," Millie said. "We'll sort it out later." She turned to Andy. "Is there anything else we should know?"

Andy glanced at his watch. "It's almost show time! You have just enough time to grab a quick bite to eat before meeting me at the passenger exit in forty-five minutes."

Millie stood and saluted her boss. "Yes sir."

Danielle and Millie headed out but not before Danielle left a parting shot. "I have no idea what I ever did to you, but whatever it was, I'm sorry."

Andy patted Danielle's shoulder. "It's nothing personal Danielle. If you and Millie want to swap tasks, I'll leave that up to you."

He followed them to the door and waited for them to step out onto the stage before closing the door.

"I'm sure the buffet is a zoo," Millie said. "Let's head down to the crew dining room."

The crew mess was as busy as Millie envisioned *Waves* buffet would be. The line snaked around the food counter, down the outer wall and to the entrance door.

There wasn't an empty seat in the place and after filling their plates, they stood at the long counter which ran along the wall.

While they ate, Millie told Danielle about the scene she'd observed right after the ship docked and how they had loaded Brody into the back of the ambulance and drove off. "Did you hear anything about a brawl on board this cruise where a passenger ended up in the clink?"

"Nope." Danielle said. "It must have been pretty bad for them to take Brody away in an ambulance."

They chatted for a few more minutes while they finished their food. Millie downed the last of her lukewarm coffee before the women carried their dirty plates to the bin near the door.

Danielle headed to the cabin to get ready while Millie hurried up the steps to deck five where the guests were lined up, patiently waiting to exit the ship.

Suharto, the ship's gangway security employee, gave the thumbs up.

Andy moved the black velvet rope off to the side and waved the first guest in line forward. "Thank you for sailing on Siren of the Seas. We can't wait for you to cruise with us again."

Several passengers stopped to ask questions about luggage, security and customs clearance. There was even a couple, still in their pajamas, who wanted to know the latest they had to vacate their cabin and exit the ship.

Hours later, the majority of the guests had "dinged" their keycards and made their way off the ship.

Millie caught a glimpse of Dave Patterson and a man who limped slowly as they boarded the ship and walked towards Donovan Sweeney's office. When the men got closer, Millie did a double take. It was an injured Brody.

Chapter 3

Millie's mouth fell open as she stared at her friend in disbelief. "Oh my gosh. Brody! What in the world happened?"

"Someone attacked Brody while he was making his rounds early this morning," Patterson replied. "He was knocked unconscious, so as a precaution I called an ambulance to take him to the hospital to be checked out. Brody twisted his ankle when he fell but other than that, the doctor gave him a clean bill of health."

Patterson nodded toward guest services. "We're going to let Donovan know we're back."

Millie watched them disappear inside Donovan's office. "That's terrible. I wonder who attacked Brody."

Another wave of passengers descended on them and Andy and Millie quickly switched back to cruise director mode.

It was another hour before the majority of the passengers had exited and only a few stragglers lingered, determined to stretch their vacation until the last possible moment.

"There's Donovan," Andy said. "I'd like to see if he has an update on what happened to Brody."

Andy hurried across the lobby to guest services where Donovan stood talking to an employee. Millie was hot on his heels. "Do you have an update on Brody's attack?"

"Follow me." Donovan waved them into his office and closed the door behind them before stepping behind his desk and easing into his chair.

"Brody was assigned to supervising the night crew for the upcoming dry dock project. According to Brody, he was patrolling one of the lower maintenance decks when he thought he heard thumping and grunting noises coming from one of the side corridors. He hurried over to investigate and said he found a man wearing a maintenance uniform. The man was sprawled out, face down on the floor. Brody said he leaned over to check on him and felt a sharp pain in the back of his head."

Donovan paused to let his words sink in. "Brody said the next thing he knew, Doctor Gundervan and several crewmembers were standing over him. They loaded him on a stretcher and took him to medical where Doctor Gundervan examined Brody. Gundervan and Patterson decided he needed to be taken to the hospital for a more thorough exam."

Millie interrupted. "What about the maintenance guy Brody found unconscious?"

Donovan shifted in his seat. "We have no idea what happened to him. Another security crewmember was the one who found Brody. He said there was no one else there. It was just Brody."

"Brody hit his head so hard, he's imagining things?" Millie lifted a hand to her lips. "That's terrible."

"Patterson has launched a full investigation," Donovan said.

"I would," Andy said. "A thug is roaming the ship and needs to be apprehended."

Andy stood. "We better head out. I need to check with Suharto to see how many guests are still on board."

They returned to the atrium and approached the gangway where Suharto informed them there were only two passengers who had still not exited the ship. "It is Kelly and Dan Avery. They are in cabin 3444."

Andy turned to Millie. "How much you wanna bet it's the two passengers who came down earlier in their pajamas?"

"I'll go light a fire," Millie said.

She left Andy and Suharto and wandered down to the main deck and to the rear of the ship. She knocked sharply on the door of cabin 3444 and waited.

Millie could've sworn she heard a muffled thump from inside the cabin so she knocked again, this time harder.

There was still no answer. "This is Millie Sanders, Assistant Cruise Director. You must vacate the ship," she hollered through the door.

"I'm coming in." Millie made good on her threat as she removed her lanyard and used her master keycard to open the cabin door.

A young couple sat lounging on the bed, munching on fruit and sipping coffee. At least they were dressed. "W-what do you think you're doing?" the young man stuttered.

"Mr. Avery," Millie said calmly. "The last call to exit the ship was over half an hour ago." She jabbed her finger at the speaker overhead. "We have been announcing final departures for over an hour now."

Avery popped a grape in his mouth and turned to the woman sitting next to him. "I didn't hear anything. Did you?"

"Uh-uh." The woman shook her head but avoided eye contact with Millie. "I had no idea."

Millie pulled her radio from her belt. "I'm going to give you precisely one minute to gather your belongings and accompany me to the gangway before I call security."

"We better go," Kelly Avery whispered.

"All right." Avery scowled at Millie as he set the half-eaten plate of food on the nightstand. "Now that you've got all our money, you're ready to toss us overboard."

"The. Cruise. Is. Over," Millie gritted between clenched teeth. "We're thrilled you loved it so much you don't want to leave but all good things must come to an end."

She watched them pick up their backpacks and Ms. Avery's purse and then waited for them to step into the hall.

The cabin steward hovered in the hall and Millie waited until the couple was several steps ahead.

Millie winked at the cabin steward and he smiled widely. "Thanks Miss Millie," he whispered and then hurried inside the empty cabin.

She personally escorted the couple to the exit and let out a sigh of relief when the couple dinged their keycards, rounded the corner and disappeared from sight.

"Good job, Millie." Andy joined her by the exit. "You have the magic touch," he teased.

"I have something all right," Millie shot back. "Magic touch? I'm not sure about that."

"What are you doing for lunch?" Andy asked.

"Is that an invitation?" Millie asked.

"Yes. There's something I'd like to discuss with you and thought we could do it over lunch." Andy placed a light arm around Millie's shoulders. "I know this fabulous little buffet restaurant not far from here."

Millie chuckled. "I hear the prices are very reasonable."

"That they are."

The captain had announced the *Waves* buffet was open to all crew and staff for lunch. The place was packed, but instead of impatient, grumbling passengers, there was a sea of smiling faces.

Although Millie, Danielle and the other entertainment staff was allowed to mix and mingle with guests in the common areas, including the dining rooms, the other crew...wait staff, housekeeping, maintenance and all other workers, were not allowed. There were times Millie felt guilty about the special privilege.

The lunch buffet boasted a feast of food - everything ranging from Italian to Greek to

Indian. Even the sushi bar was open and loaded with an array of dishes.

Millie wasn't a fan of sushi and it was probably a good thing. The line was long...longer than the buffet line.

She eased a wedge of lasagna, a thick slice of roasted turkey, a piece of crispy fried chicken onto her plate and topped it with a crusty roll.

She squeezed into a corner table for two and waited for Andy, whose plate was piled high with fries, a greasy cheeseburger and a chilidog. He'd even managed to fit a slice of pepperoni pizza on the plate and it teetered precariously on top of the mountain of food.

"You must not be very hungry." Millie grinned.

Andy placed the plate on the table and patted his stomach. "I decided to go for a light lunch. I'm trying to watch my girlish figure."

He slid into the chair opposite Millie and waited while she silently prayed before unfolding his silverware and placing his napkin in his lap.

Andy's expression grew serious. "There's something I'd like to talk to you about."

Chapter 4

Millie's first thought was that she was on the chopping block but quickly dismissed it. Surely, Nic would've given her a heads up if that were the case, unless he didn't know.

"My mum has taken a tumble back home. She's staying with my sister, Sarah, right now but we're going to be moving her from the family home to a care home."

"I'm sorry to hear that." Millie reached out and touched Andy's hand.

"I know that it's short notice, but I've booked a flight to the UK. It leaves early Saturday morning, the day Siren of the Seas sets sail for its first voyage after the dry dock."

"Is someone going to fill in for you while you're off?"

Andy shifted in his seat. "That's where you come in, Millie. I've talked to Donovan and Captain Armati and we all agree you can cover for me for the couple of weeks I'll be gone."

The blood drained from Millie's face. "Me?" she squeaked. "Andy. I can't fill your shoes."

"Yes, you can," Andy insisted. "Remember when I got food poisoning and was laid up? You handled my job like you'd been doing it for years."

"It was for one day. Not a couple of weeks." Millie briefly closed her eyes. Of course, she knew almost all of the onboard activities like the back of her hand, but there were other things Andy did Millie had no idea about. "I want to help, Andy. Really, I do."

"Great." Andy cut her off. "I knew I could count on you." He bit the end of his pizza and smiled between bites. "Danielle will be moving up to take your place during my absence."

"You're kidding," Millie said.

"She's stepped up to the plate the last couple of months, especially while you were on break. Danielle can handle it."

"She might be able to handle my job but I'm not so sure I can handle Danielle," Millie groaned.

"You'll be fine. I'll be back before you know it."

There was no way Millie wanted Andy to feel guilty for returning home to care for his mother. She would've done the same thing had she been in his shoes. In fact, Millie and her older brother had dealt with a similar situation when they discovered their mother, Grace, no longer remembered who they were.

It had been a sad time in Millie's life and her mother had lived only a couple years inside a nursing facility before passing on.

Grace had hated every minute of it, missed her home and Millie couldn't blame her, but she also couldn't care for her mother 24/7.

Millie pasted a smile on her face. "You're right, Andy. Don't worry about a thing. Danielle and I, along with all of the other amazing entertainment staff, will keep things humming along." She wagged her finger at him. "But don't be getting any ideas. If you don't come back, I'll hunt you down."

"I have no doubt you will," Andy said. They finished their food and after taking care of their dirty dishes, made their way onto the empty lido deck.

Millie wrinkled her nose at the overpowering fumes of floor cleaner that filled the air. Several crewmembers were hard at work stripping and sanding the floorboards behind the lido bar area. "I'm going to run up to the bridge to talk to N-Captain Armati and after that I'll start on my to-do list."

"Now that you're on board with covering for me while I'm gone, I'll have a chat with Danielle," Andy said.

"Be sure to tell her she has to behave," Millie said.

"Will do." Andy gave her a thumbs up.

Millie watched as he strolled to the other side of the deck and descended the steps. "This ought to be interesting," she muttered under her breath.

Millie slipped inside the empty bridge and caught a glimpse of Craig McMasters, the ship's first officer. He was standing on the bridge deck gazing out at the dock below. The door was open and she tiptoed across the floor.

Millie cleared her throat when she got closer.

"Millie." McMasters turned, a smile lighting his face. "I hear y'ear gettin' to be the big dog on the upcomin' cruise," he teased in his thick Scottish accent.

"It looks like I have no choice," Millie said. "Sink or swim. Hopefully I do the latter."

"You'll do great, lass," he said confidently and then nodded toward Captain Armati's private apartment behind the bridge. "The captain just took a wee break to check on Scout."

"Thanks." Millie made her way across the bridge and down the small hall to the captain's door where she rapped lightly.

When the door opened, Scout, the captain's teacup Yorkie, barreled out of the apartment and pounced on Millie's shoe. She bent down to pick him up and held him close as he pawed her chin. "You act as if you haven't seen me in days." She nuzzled him close before setting him on the floor where he promptly darted into the bridge to greet Officer McMasters.

"Millie," the captain said in a soft voice. "I was just getting ready to call you to invite you to dinner later this evening."

"I'll have to run it by Andy but since we no longer have passengers on board, I don't see it being a problem."

"Excellent. I've been in the kitchen picking up a few tips from Amit and have a special dinner in mind."

"You're making dinner?"

"Are you surprised?" he asked.

"No. I mean, yes," she admitted.

"Don't worry. We can always order room service if it doesn't turn out," he teased.

Scout flew back down the hall and skidded to a halt between them.

"Would you like to come in for a moment?" He opened the door wider and waited for Millie to step inside.

"I hope I'm not bothering you," Millie said. "I should've called first."

"No bother." Nic moved close and snaked his arm around her waist.

Millie wrapped her arms around his neck and closed her eyes as he leaned forward to kiss her.

She began to feel lightheaded and when the kiss ended, Millie let out a shallow breath as she pressed the palms of her hands against her flushed cheeks. "Many more kisses like that and we'll have to ask Pastor Evans to marry us."

"I can see if he's free now."

"Very funny." Millie decided to switch to a safer subject lest she throw caution to the wind and take him up on the suggestion. "Andy told me about his leave to return home."

"Yes, I heard. You'll do a fine job, Millie."

They chatted for several moments as Millie expressed her concerns, all of which Nic dismissed in an attempt to convince her she would breeze through the two weeks.

A light tap on the door ended the conversation.

"I better get back to work," Millie said.

"Sorry to bother you Captain," McMasters apologized. "They're calling for you from the engine room."

"I'll be right there." Nic accompanied her out of the apartment and to the bridge door. "So I'll see you at six for dinner?"

"Of course." Millie smiled. "I can't wait." She waved good-bye to Officer McMasters and headed to the karaoke stage to start sorting through the songs.

Zack Smythe, one of the dancers, was perched on a barstool, a playlist in hand.

"You're here to work on the list, too?" Millie asked.

"Yep." Zack nodded. "I say we create an 'oldies but goodies' folder and put anything that hasn't been requested in the last six months in the book."

"Good idea." Millie hurried over to the guest services desk to borrow a blank sheet of paper and ink pen. When she returned, she pulled up a stool and hopped on top. "We can also start a list of recent passenger requests we don't have on hand."

The two of them began working on moving, modifying and adding to the playlist. Millie was surprised by how many newer songs guests never selected and how many classics they seemed to love.

Dave Patterson wandered into the atrium and Millie did a double take. Concern over Brody's attack lingered in the back of her mind. She'd been praying for her young friend off and on since hearing about the incident.

"I'll be right back." Millie slid off the stool and hurried to the other side of the room. "How's Brody?"

"Brody is resting in his cabin." Patterson's shoulders sagged. "He swears up and down he saw someone sprawled out on a lower corridor floor, right before someone attacked him from behind."

"Maybe the person had some sort of seizure and came to, got scared when they saw Brody on the ground unconscious and took off," Millie said.

"Or Brody's mind is playing tricks on him," Patterson said. "I made him take the rest of the day off."

Patterson stared blankly at Millie. "There was one thing I noticed at the scene that doesn't make sense."

"What's that?"

"It was a…" Patterson stopped abruptly. "It was nothing. Forget I ever said anything."

"You have to tell me now," Millie insisted. "That's not fair."

Patterson sucked in a breath. "There was a small puddle of blood next to Brody and Brody wasn't bleeding."

"So it's possible Brody did see someone lying on the floor. What about surveillance cameras?"

"We have cameras in the main corridors but the incident took place in a smaller, side corridor," Patterson said. "I'm on my way to talk to Doctor Gundervan, to see if any crewmembers visited the medical center around the time of Brody's attack."

Millie returned to the karaoke area to finish her project while Dave Patterson strode to the bank of elevators.

Zack waited until Millie settled onto her seat. "Word around the ship is the 'Bro-meister' was attacked last night."

Millie frowned.

"Brody," Zack clarified.

"Yeah. It's terrible. He never saw his attacker."

Zack shook his head. "I don't know why the maintenance guys keep messin' with Brody. The dude could knock them out with the swipe of his hand."

Chapter 5

"Are you saying Brody has been attacked before?" Millie was surprised. It was the first she'd heard of anyone not liking Brody. In fact, he was one of her favorites. He reminded her of her son, Blake.

"He got that big promo as head of night security and since then, I've heard a couple times he's gotten into it with the crew."

Millie frowned. "Do you think he's on a power trip, maybe rubbing some of the crew the wrong way and they're attacking him?" she asked.

Zack shrugged. "I dunno. He never struck me as that kind of person but then you know him better than I do."

The two of them finished going through the playlist but all the while Millie mulled over what Zack had said. Maybe Brody's promotion *had* gone to his head and he was bullying other crew.

He'd always seemed even-tempered to Millie, except for the time Andy tased him during a demonstration and Brody grabbed the Taser from Andy and turned it back on him. Millie grinned as she remembered the incident.

It still didn't explain Brody's insistence he'd stumbled upon an unconscious man right before his attack and Patterson's comment about the puddle of blood.

After Millie and Zack finished their karaoke project, Millie wandered to the theater to check on Danielle, who had said she was going to get the bingo ball project out of the way first.

Muffled voices echoed from behind the stage curtain as Millie made her way up the steps. She caught a glimpse of Danielle inside the dancer's dressing room.

"How's the bingo ball project progressing?"

Danielle spun around, the B15 ball in her hand. "Just fabulous." She reached inside the bingo ball cage and pulled one out, holding it up. "Do you see a difference?"

Millie caught a hint of sarcasm in Danielle's voice. "Yes, as a matter of fact I do. The B15 looks brand new. Let's talk swap. Do you want to inventory and repair costumes and I'll inventory the books and board games in the library?"

"I thought you'd never ask," Danielle said. "Speaking of asking have you heard anything on Brody's condition?"

Millie relayed what Patterson had told her. "How well do you know Brody?"

Danielle dropped the clean ball into the cage and picked up another one. "We've talked a few times. I had that minor incident up in the casino the time I tried to sneak behind the cashier's counter and he got onto me. I see him in the employee lounge once in a while if things get a little out of hand. Why?"

"Because Zack said since Brody was promoted to head of night security, he's had a few run-ins with some of the night crew."

"I haven't heard that," Danielle said. "He seems pretty laid back. Maybe he's on a power trip since his promotion."

Millie had a hard time believing it. Brody didn't seem the type, but then again, maybe he acted differently around her.

Even if that was the case, she hoped he was going to be all right. Millie wondered if Patterson had heard the rumors. She quickly decided to stay out of it...for once. Brody was an adult. If he wanted to go after his attacker or attackers, it was his decision.

She headed to the library to start her cataloguing assignment and as Millie walked from one end of the ship to the other, she was again struck by how odd it was for the ship to be passenger-free.

Millie used her master key to unlock the library door. She stepped inside the cozy room and closed the door behind her.

The library was small and intimate, and although there were a wide variety of books ranging from traditional mystery, to romance and even boasted a few biographies, the selection was limited.

Millie closed her eyes and savored the quiet, breathing in the lingering smell of well-worn books. With her busy schedule, she rarely had the luxury of borrowing one of the library books, settling into a comfy chair and losing herself in a good story.

While Danielle hated the library and thought it boring, Millie loved it. Books could transport one to such wonderful places and had many times taken her on some amazing adventures.

She turned the lights and computer on, and headed to the first cabinet to begin working on the inventory.

The time flew by as Millie immersed herself in the task and she even found several books she longed to read. Maybe someday...maybe on her honeymoon, she would have time to read.

Nic and Millie had discussed traveling to his hometown of Bertoli, a quaint village on the shores of the Mediterranean Sea, for their honeymoon.

She'd never traveled abroad, except on board the cruise ship, and was excited at the prospect, but first Captain Armati and she had to overcome one large obstacle, which was Majestic Cruise Line's policy.

Danielle had suggested starting a petition to collect crew and staff signatures, asking the cruise line to grant a special allowance for the couple.

Several people had told Millie there was no way the cruise line would allow for their marriage but she refused to accept that, not until she had it in writing. She'd prayed about it every morning when she woke. God would not have brought Nic into her life just to break her heart.

Millie pushed the thought aside as she finished inventorying the first bookcase. The pages were starting to blur, her signal it was time to give her eyes a rest so she shut the computer off and exited the library.

Millie slowed as she passed by *Ocean Treasures,* the ship's gift shop. Cat was inside, surrounded by a wall of boxes and empty shelves.

Cat caught Millie's eye and motioned to her as she hurried to the door to unlock it.

"You're up to your eyeballs in rum cake." Millie tapped her finger on top of a gold-colored box labeled *Tortuga Caribbean Chocolate Rum Cake.*

"I thought revamping the store would be fun but I'm feeling a little overwhelmed." Cat pushed a stray strand of jet black hair from her eyes. "What are you up to?"

"Library inventory," Millie said.

Cat wrinkled her nose. "Yuck. That would be like torture."

"You sound like Danielle. I swapped her library inventory task for my costume inventory."

"Now that would be much more interesting." Cat shifted one of the shelves to the side. "I've decided to venture off the ship while we're here."

"Good for you Cat. So you're going to accompany Annette and me while I shop for a wedding dress?"

"Yeah. One day this week Joe and I are going to do a little sightseeing and shopping near the port and maybe stop by South Beach."

Millie had never visited South Beach, although she'd heard some things about it from several other crewmembers who had been there. It wasn't exactly Millie's 'cup of tea.'

"Tara, one of the dancers, told me South Beach is a hot spot for Miami's rich and famous." She changed the subject. "Friday would be a good day for dress shopping. I'll try to track down a few shops close to the port. We can make a day of it and enjoy a lunch on the water, too. My treat for dragging you along."

"Sounds good. I better get back to work if I want to get this joint put back together before Saturday." Cat walked Millie to the door. "Did you hear about the poor security guard who was attacked?"

Cat was talking about Brody. "Yeah. Brody Rourke. He's a good guy. I guess he's had a couple run-ins with crew lately. He was recently promoted to head of night security. I'd like to stop by and tell him I'm glad he's okay but I have no idea where his cabin is."

"I can find out for you." Cat retraced her steps as she hurried to the computer and cash register near the back of the store.

Millie followed behind and watched as Cat swiped her ID card along the side of the computer screen and then tapped the keys as she squinted at the screen. "It looks like he just switched cabins. He's in C187."

"That's one deck up from my cabin." Millie thanked Cat for the information and wandered out of the store.

She swung by the galley to chat with Annette. Millie stuck her head in the round galley window that reminded her of a porthole. She spotted her friend in the middle of the kitchen, surrounded by the kitchen staff so she kept going.

Instead of heading back to the library, she headed below deck, to the crew computer area, which was empty.

Millie eased into a seat near the back before logging on. The internet moved at lightning speed, one of the upsides of being in port and not in the middle of the ocean.

She quickly checked her bank account before moving onto her email and finally researching local bridal shops and restaurants close to the port.

Millie jotted several names and addresses down before logging off. She stopped by her cabin to drop off the bridal shop and restaurant info, tucking them off to the side of the desk. Millie wondered if she should invite Danielle to tag along on the shopping trip. Danielle had made a few friends on board but none Millie would categorize as 'close' friends.

The young woman had been on the ship for almost a year now and Millie still knew very little about her past life or her family. Danielle had told Millie she'd once worked full time as an undercover agent and also as an archaeologist.

The careers struck Millie as polar opposites but that was Danielle. The young woman marched to the beat of her own drum.

There was also the mystery of Danielle's brother, Casey, who had died. On more than one occasion, Danielle confessed to Millie she blamed herself for her brother's death.

Millie quickly decided to include Danielle, if Andy would allow them both to be off the ship at the same time. She remembered how she had agreed to cover for Andy while he returned home to care for his mother. Andy owed her one so it wouldn't hurt to ask.

She flipped off the cabin light and stepped into the hall, deciding to stop by Brody's cabin to check on him before grabbing lunch and returning to the library.

C187 was one deck up and near the back or aft of the ship, directly above Dave Patterson's office, if Millie's guess was correct.

The upper crew deck was smaller than the crew area below and included just the back section of the ship. Passenger cabins filled the front or forward section.

She strode to the back and easily located the cabin. Millie lifted her hand to knock when she noticed a folded piece of paper tucked in the door. There was something scrawled on the outside and she tilted her head to read it. "Brody."

Thinking someone had left a card for Brody, she plucked it out. The word "lucky" caught Millie's eye. The temptation was too great so she unfolded the note:

Next time you won't be so lucky.

Chapter 6

Millie quickly folded the note, unsure of whether she should show it to Brody. She knocked on his cabin door but no one answered so she tried again. There was still no answer.

She had two choices...to put the note back where she found it or take it to Patterson. Clearly, Brody was being targeted and Patterson needed to know.

Millie hurried down the corridor to the stairs and descended one level, to where Patterson's office was located. She tapped lightly and heard a muffled reply. Hoping that meant come in, she turned the knob and stepped inside.

Dave Patterson was behind his desk. Sitting across from him was Oscar and Donovan Sweeney. Each wore a serious expression on their face.

"I hope I'm not interrupting," she apologized.

Donovan stood. "I was just getting ready to leave."

"Me too." Oscar joined him.

"Wait." Millie held up a hand. "I have something to show you. It's about Brody."

Oscar and Patterson exchanged an uneasy glance and Millie had a sneaking suspicion their meeting had been about Brody.

She handed the note to Patterson, who glanced at the front and then unfolded the paper. He read the brief note before handing it to Donovan.

Millie studied Donovan's expression. "It sounds like a threat to me."

Donovan folded the note and set it on Patterson's desk. "Where did you find this?"

"I stopped by Brody's cabin to check on him. He wasn't there but I found this note tucked in his door. I didn't mean to look at it but the paper is thin and I could read a couple of the words."

"Curiosity killed the cat," Donovan said. "Brody is at a safety meeting. They're going over safety with the maintenance crew and temporary crew for the dry dock work being done. I'm going to assign Brody to guard the exit gate, to check ID's coming into the docking area."

"Someone is out to get Brody," Millie said. "Rumor has it this isn't the first incident. He's gotten into a couple scuffles since moving to nightshift and heading night security."

Patterson leaned back in his chair and ran his hand through his hair. "I'm aware of the other instances. Brody swears these were unprovoked attacks."

"Have you talked to the crewmember who found Brody unconscious?" Millie asked. She thought about the person Brody claimed he saw lying on the floor.

"I have," Donovan said. "He knows as much as we do. That Brody was unconscious and there was no one else around."

"The easiest solution is to move Brody back to days but it will be a demotion and so far, he's shrugging everything off, like it's no big deal," Patterson added. "I don't get it."

"You may have to demote him for his own good." Oscar, who had so far remained silent, spoke. "I like Brody. He seems like a good guy and a hard worker. I don't understand."

"Maybe he thinks the problem was solved last night," Millie added.

After Millie left Patterson's office, she headed upstairs to grab a bite to eat. The lunch crowd had already cleared out and there were only a few stragglers wandering around. Millie settled on a bowl of soup and carried her tray to a table overlooking the bay.

After praying over her food and adding a special prayer for Brody, she crumbled her crackers, sprinkled them into her soup and reached for her spoon.

"There you are." Annette appeared, carrying a tray laden with baked chicken, chicken wings, fried chicken and a roll.

"Chicken?" Millie grinned as she pointed the tip of her soupspoon at Annette's plate.

"Yeah. I'm experimenting with some new chicken recipes but needed a refresher on what the current recipes taste like." Annette transferred the plate from the tray to the table and set the empty tray on the seat next to her before she plopped down and pulled a notepad and pen from her pocket.

"You weren't kidding," Millie said.

"Food is serious business on a cruise ship," Annette said as she reached for a chicken wing. "I'm thinking of adding a honey barbecue chicken to the menu."

"I love chicken wings," Millie said.

Annette bit into a drumette and then waved it at Millie's soup. "Dieting for the dress?"

"No. I'm worried about Brody," Millie confessed.

"Brody?"

"Brody Rourke. He's head of night security. You may remember him from the tasing demonstration awhile back."

Annette snorted. "Oh yeah. Him. Is he the guy who got jumped? Amit said he heard some security guy was attacked and they took him to the hospital."

"Yeah, that was him." Millie went on to explain how Brody had gotten into a few minor scuffles with night crew. "Brody claims he was making his rounds and stumbled upon a maintenance worker in one of the hallways, lying on the floor. He leaned over to check on him and the next thing he knew, Doctor Gundervan was hovering over him. Someone had attacked him from behind and knocked him out."

"What happened to the other guy?" Annette asked.

"That's the odd part. When one of the crewmembers found Brody unconscious on the floor, it was only Brody lying there. There was no one else."

"Bodies don't just vanish," Annette said. "Maybe the guy passed out and when he came to he saw Brody, panicked and ran off."

"That's what I thought, too." Millie lowered her voice. "Patterson said there was a small pool of blood next to Brody and it wasn't his."

Annette arched a brow. "Interesting. So maybe there was someone there, just like Brody said."

Millie nodded and then told Annette about the note she found tucked in Brody's cabin door.

"Sounds like he's in for another round," Annette said. "Patterson knows about it?"

"Yeah. So does Donovan. They'll have to do something." Millie sipped her soup and then set the spoon on the table. "I've got it. Remember the electrical fire that killed Luigi Falco, the electrician?"

"Yeah."

"Well, I got to know Marcus, one of the other electricians when he helped me set up Killer Karaoke in the atrium. He works around maintenance. I wonder if he knows what's going on."

On the one hand, Millie wondered if she should just mind her own business. Brody hadn't asked for her help. Patterson wouldn't appreciate her sticking her nose in where it didn't belong. She doubted the crew would be forthcoming when questioned by the ship's officers. She, on the other hand, was more on their level.

Plus, Marcus owed her one, in a roundabout way.

"Try this wingette and tell me what's missing." Annette dropped a small chicken wing on Millie's plate.

Millie tore off a piece of meat and popped it in her mouth. "It's missing the zip. The buffalo sauce is a little bland."

"My sentiments exactly." Annette shook her head. "I keep telling the cooks to skip the curry powder and add more cayenne pepper and hot sauce but they won't do it."

"Yeah, now that you mention it, I can taste the curry." Millie finished the wing and her soup and glanced at her watch. "Are you free Friday to do some dress shopping and lunch? My treat."

"Sure."

"I've already invited Cat and plan to invite Danielle."

"It will be nice to get off the ship," Annette said.

Millie waited until Annette finished her food and then stood. "I'll see if I can track down Marcus before I head back to the library to work on the inventory."

Andy had given Danielle and Millie flexible schedules. As long as they finished the tasks on their lists before Saturday, he told them they could work at their own pace.

"I need to check on the clean-up crew working on the walk-in coolers." Annette gave a small wave and climbed the side stairs.

Millie headed down the steps and the direction she hoped was the electrical department. She'd toured the area once, months ago, and vaguely remembered it was close to the engineering and mechanical departments.

The engineering and mechanical departments were off limits to everyone except the crew who worked in those departments but with Millie's clearance level, she was able to access the restricted areas.

As she descended below water level and the stairwell narrowed, her claustrophobia kicked in, causing her to pause halfway. "You can do this," she whispered under her breath and forced herself to continue her descent.

When she reached the narrow hall, she turned left, in the direction she hoped was the electrical department. Several curved metal doors lined the corridor and when she passed the one marked *Engineering* she knew she was getting close. She passed the engine room and on the other side, she finally found what she was looking for.

While the other doors were solid metal, the door leading to the electrical department sported a small, square window with a thick layer of glass. Thin strips of wire crisscrossed the glass.

The window was slightly higher than eye level. Millie bounced on the tips of her toes in an attempt to see inside. The room was tiny and crammed full of equipment.

Her claustrophobia level inched toward a full-scale, heart pounding red alert and she began to feel lightheaded.

Determined to find out what Marcus might know, she shoved her rising panic aside and rapped sharply on the outer door.

A man's face appeared in the window, a face Millie didn't recognize. The door opened just far enough for him to peer out. "Can I help you?"

"I'm looking for Marcus," Millie said.

"Marcus not here," the man answered in a thick Spanish accent. "He up in the theater working on stage equipment."

"Thank goodness." Millie pressed a hand to her chest; more than a little relieved she wouldn't have to enter the miniscule space. "Thank you."

The man mumbled something and the door closed. She heard a "click" as he locked the door behind him.

"You don't have to worry about me trying to break into your cave." Millie spun on her heel and retraced her steps. She hurried up the stairs and by the time she reached deck three, the first floor of the theater, she had to stop to catch her breath.

The doors to the theater were closed, and Millie could hear the low rumble of music coming from within.

Millie stepped inside and climbed the side stairs to the second level where the sound booth and stage lighting was located. Crammed inside the confined booth were several crewmembers.

There was a blinding flash of bright light and Millie caught a glimpse of Marcus, right in the thick of things. She shielded her eyes and pressed her forehead against the clear Plexiglas as she tried to catch his eye.

The workers either didn't notice her or were ignoring her so Millie began waving her arms wildly.

Finally, one of the men opened the door.

"I need to speak with Marcus."

"Sure." The man tapped Marcus' shoulder and pointed toward Millie.

Marcus pulled a headset off his head and wove his way past several workers. "Miss Millie."

"Hi Marcus. I'm sorry to bother you, but wondered if you had a minute to talk."

"Yes, of course." Marcus glanced over his shoulder. "I'll be back." He stepped out of the booth and closed the door behind him. "Don't tell me you found more hot wires."

"No, thank goodness," Millie said. "I try to avoid electrical components whenever possible."

Marcus followed Millie out of the theater and into the hall. She decided to get right to the point. "Did you hear about Brody Rourke's attack last night?"

"Yes." Marcus nodded. "Everyone knows."

"I figured. So what's your take on what happened?"

Marcus averted his gaze and shuffled his feet, a sure sign he knew something.

"I...uh."

"You know something," Millie said. "Please, tell me so I can help Brody."

"The night maintenance, they don't like Brody," Marcus finally said.

"I know that," Millie said. "What I don't know is why. Is he bullying people?"

"No."

"Does he have dirt on someone and they're trying to get rid of him?"

"I don't think so." Marcus shook his head.

Millie almost told Marcus about the note but kept quiet. She wasn't supposed to know about it. "I don't think last night was the end of Brody's harassment. I think it's going to continue."

Marcus shifted his feet. "It would be best if he work days. Like I said, the night crew, they don't like him."

"Why?" Millie pressed.

"I don't know for certain. I do know during our last cruise, right after the port stop in San Juan, the crew began to say they no want Brody on the ship."

"But you don't know why?"

"No Miss Millie," Marcus said. "They like Brody and joke around with him but after the stop in San Juan, I hear rumors they going to get rid of him. I thought they were just talking until last night."

"Have you heard anything today, any new news about getting rid of Brody?" Millie asked.

"No, but I've been up here working since early this morning. If anyone knows what is going on downstairs, it would be Sharky."

"Sharky?"

"He runs the crew, you know the dock workers, forklift drivers. He's the unofficial head honcho below the water line."

"So you think Sharky is the person I should talk to?" Millie asked.

Marcus shook his head. "No. I'm not telling you to go to the water line. It's a different world down there. I'm just saying if anyone knows what happened to Brody, it would be Sharky."

"Say I did want to talk to Sharky. Is it safe?"

"I wouldn't go down there alone," Marcus said. "Sharky - he work the day shift but one of his men, he is in charge at night."

"What about Frank Bauer? I thought Frank was the head of maintenance?" Millie asked.

"Yes, on paper, but Frank, he doesn't have time to oversee every department so he turns a blind eye to Sharky's pull."

Millie believed Marcus was telling her the truth. "That sheds a little light on the situation. So say I wanted to find Sharky. Where do I look?"

"Storage area block 'A' or 'B'. I've seen him in both. He also has an office down there. It has his name on the door."

"What does Sharky look like?"

"You can't miss him. He rides around on a black scooter," Marcus said.

Millie thanked Marcus for sharing what he knew and promised she wouldn't tell anyone what she'd heard from him.

"You're welcome, Miss Millie. Be careful if you decide to track Sharky down." Marcus reached for the door handle. "I like Brody. He's a good guy but I think he should switch to the day shift." He didn't wait for a reply as he stepped back inside the theater and the door closed behind him.

Chapter 7

"So you're saying Marcus heard something went down during our last port stop in San Juan and it triggered the violence toward Brody?" Annette asked.

"Yep. Up until that night, the night crew had no problem with Brody." Millie glanced around the galley and lowered her voice. "I hope Patterson was able to convince Brody to give up the night shift, even if only temporarily until they can figure out why he's being targeted."

Cat tapped the tip of her nail on the stainless steel counter. "I haven't seen Brody myself but Joe said he took a hard fall." She shivered. "If someone on board this ship is still bent on hurting him, he could be in danger."

"Last I heard, he was fighting taking time off and plans to show up for his shift at the guard gate tonight," Danielle said.

Millie told the women about Sharky, the maintenance supervisor who worked the day shift.

"I've never heard of the man," Cat said.

"I have," Danielle said. "I always wondered who he was. The bartenders in the employee lounge like to tease the rowdies that if they don't straighten up, they're going to send them downstairs to work for Sharky."

"I wouldn't mind having a word with Sharky," Millie said. "I mean, how bad can he be?"

"I'll go with you," Danielle offered.

"No." Annette shook her head.

"Why not?"

"Danielle, look at you. You would stand out like a sore thumb," Annette said. "If Millie goes down there, we need to keep it on the down low, or as down low as we can. I'll go."

She turned to Millie. "I've heard of Sharky. Rumor has it he's one tough cookie."

Wisps of smoke drifted from both corners of the nearby oven and caught Millie's eye. "Something is burning."

"Chicken!" Annette grabbed a potholder and flung the oven door open.

A large plume of smoke filled the air and Annette waved the potholder in a desperate attempt to clear the air. "Amit!"

She pulled the tray from the oven rack and slid it onto the counter. "We got lucky. It's just a little grease burning off."

Amit flew through the galley door. "I forgot about my chicken!"

"You almost burned the place down," Annette teased. "Where did you wander off to?"

"I was up in the captain's apartment. He working on a special dinner."

All eyes turned to Millie.

"Let me guess, Captain Armati is making you dinner," Cat said.

Millie's cheeks warmed. "Yeah. What are we having?" She turned to Amit.

"Oh no Miss Millie." Amit shook his head. "It a surprise. A good surprise. You be very happy."

"Oh I'm sure she will," Danielle teased. "Must be nice having the captain of the ship make dinner for you."

"He offered," Millie said lamely. "I couldn't turn him down."

"Speaking of which, any news on Majestic Cruise Lines bending the rules and letting you two lovebirds tie the knot?" Annette asked.

"No." With Brody's current dilemma, Millie had almost forgotten about her own. Almost.

"I say we move full steam ahead and start a petition," Danielle said.

"Me too," Cat agreed.

"I think we're going to need all the help we can get." Millie slid off her chair. "I better check in with Andy before I get ready for dinner."

"Have fun," Danielle teased. "Don't do anything I wouldn't do."

***

Millie found Andy in the dressing room, rifling through the makeup bags. Propped up on the counter in front of him was a large clipboard. "How's it going?"

Andy, whose back was to the door, jumped. "You scared me half to death."

"Sorry," Millie said. "You're inventorying the stage makeup?"

"Yeah." Andy shook his head. "This stuff seems to grow legs and just walk away."

He changed the subject. "What have you been up to all day?"

Millie gave him a rundown of what she'd accomplished, which wasn't as much as she'd hoped, having been sidetracked by Brody's situation. "I finished half the library book inventory and should have it finished by late tomorrow morning. Zack and I updated the playlist for karaoke and ordered some new music."

"It sounds like you accomplished a lot," Andy said. "Do you still plan to shop in Miami?" She told him she did and that she wanted to invite Danielle to join her and the others.

"I see no problem with both of you taking some time off," Andy said. "It's rare you women get an opportunity to go out and do girly stuff."

"Plus, you owe me one," Millie reminded him.

"That I do," Andy agreed. "They're opening the dining room to the crew for dinner tonight."

"Wow. They're going all out for the crew while we're in dry dock."

"A happy crew is a hardworking crew."

"True." She glanced at her watch. "I won't be there, which reminds me I have a dinner date at six so I'll see you later."

***

Millie arrived at Nic's apartment right on time. She thought about bringing him a gift, to thank him for making dinner. Flowers seemed a little silly and so did chocolate. It wasn't as if she could run to the shopping center around the corner and pick something up.

In the end, she decided she was the gift that kept on giving and showed up on his doorstep empty-handed.

Nic had dimmed the lights and the candles in the center of the small dining room table cast the room in a romantic glow. Soft music played in the background and the smell of freshly baked bread filled the small apartment.

"Dinner is almost ready." Nic bent forward and kissed Millie tenderly before he reluctantly took a step back. "I must get the bread before it burns." He disappeared into the kitchen and Millie trailed behind. "Can I help?"

"No. It is almost ready." He pulled a baking tray from the oven, placed the pan on top and shut the oven off. "All I have left is to put these in a basket and dinner is ready."

"At least let me pour the drinks," Millie offered.

Nic grinned. "Okay, dear. Our choices are blackberry or pomegranate sparkling water. They're chilling in the refrigerator."

Millie reached inside the fridge and pulled out two bottles of blackberry water, filled two goblets with ice and then poured the carbonated beverage in the glasses. She took a sip. "This is good."

Nic eased the last piece of bread inside the basket and carried it to the table while Millie carried their drinks.

"Where's Scout?" She'd been so distracted by Nic's kiss and helping him finish dinner, she'd forgotten about the small pup.

"He kept tripping me up, begging for treats so I put him in the bedroom upstairs. I'll let him out after we eat." Nic made his way to the other side of the table and pulled out Millie's chair.

Millie eased into the seat and slid forward. "I feel guilty you went to all this trouble and I can't do the same."

"It's okay, Millie." Nic slid into his chair and reached for his silverware. "Someday, when you take me to Michigan to visit, I will let you cook for me."

"It's a deal."

During dinner, they discussed the dry dock project. Millie briefly told him of the assignments

Andy had given her. They also talked about the upcoming wedding. They still hadn't set a date since everything hinged on Majestic Cruise Lines.

Nic told Millie he was working on a special request with his own letters of support from the ship's officers.

Millie's throat clogged as he told her how the officers were thrilled for the two of them and promised they would help in any way possible. Between the staff, crew and ship's officers, how could the 'powers that be' turn them down?

She was too full for dessert so Nic brewed a pot of coffee while Millie let Scout out of the bedroom. The three of them wandered onto the balcony, overlooking the port.

It was getting dark and Millie's eyes wandered to the back of the ship. The entire area was a beehive of activity as forklifts darted back and forth, carrying supplies on board the ship.

Near one end of the gated area was a tall wall with colorful blocks dotting one side. "What's that?"

Nic followed her gaze. "It's the new rock wall. It will be installed up on the sports deck soon. Tomorrow I think."

"I remember Andy mentioning the rock-climbing wall plus some new hot tubs."

"Yes. Those will be installed this week as well." Nic's eyes twinkled. "We should try them out."

Millie's face warmed. Nic had seen her in a bathing suit one other time, the day they'd spent on a secluded Caribbean island...the day he'd proposed. "I-I would like that." She remembered thinking how muscular he'd looked without his shirt and was certain he must work out at the gym in his free time, whenever that was.

The warmth in her face crept through the rest of her body and she forced herself to focus on something other than how close he was and what he looked like without his shirt on.

Several security workers walked around the enclosed area. They were carrying clipboards and Millie assumed they were checking the worker's clearance.

"The forklift drivers..."

"Stevedores," Captain Armati nodded.

"Stevedores?"

"Stevedores are workers who load and unload cargo from the ship."

"I see." Millie nodded. "Are the stevedores employed by Siren of the Seas?" She thought of Sharky.

"No. Most are hired by the port. Because of the ship remodel, we've had to hire temporary workers to make sure the work is completed on schedule." Nic pointed to one of the security guards. "The security guards are checking their paperwork to make sure the workers are on the list."

Millie's mind drifted to Brody's attack. What if Brody had stumbled on the scene of a crime, and there really had been a body on the floor? If there really had been a person, what had happened to them?

Nic refilled their coffee cups. When he returned, he was carrying them and an assortment of small desserts including white chocolate, which was Millie's favorite. "Thank you." She plucked a treat from the plate and nibbled the corner. "Did you make these too?"

Nic set the plate on the small table next to a lounge chair. "No Millie. Unfortunately, these are beyond my limited level of expertise."

Millie sipped her coffee before polishing off her sweet treat of white chocolate and cheesecake. "Everything was delicious. I'm sure I gained at least five pounds."

"Captain Armati, do you copy?" Always on duty, the captain pulled his radio from his belt clip. "This is Captain Armati."

"Captain. This is Frank Bauer. I was wondering if I could have a word with you."

"Of course. I'm in the bridge."

"I'll be right there."

"I guess that's our signal our dinner date is over." Millie reached for her coffee cup and caught a glimpse of one of the security guards as he limped across the dock area and made his way to the entrance gate. It was Brody.

Millie and the captain barely had enough time to clear the table before there was a light tap on the apartment door.

Nic pulled Millie close and kissed her hard. "I got ripped off."

"So did I," Millie shot back as she followed him to the door.

Staff Captain Antonio Vitale stood on the other side. "I'm sorry captain. Frank Bauer said you were meeting him here." He smiled apologetically at Millie.

"Yes. We were just finishing dinner." Nic followed Millie from the apartment and closed the door behind him.

Frank stood off to one side and nodded as Captain Armati and Millie made their way to the exit.

"Thank you for a wonderful dinner."

"You're welcome my dear."

As soon as the door closed, Millie's mind switched gears. It was time to check on Brody.

Chapter 8

Millie hurried to deck one and the open gangway. She dinged her card and smiled at the crewmember manning the station.

The sun had already set and overhead floodlights beamed across the expanse of the loading dock.

The steady beep from the forklifts echoed in the cool evening air and Millie picked up the pace as two dockworkers eyed her curiously.

She briefly wondered if she should have brought someone with her but pushed the thought aside. Millie was within the safety and security of the gate so she shouldn't have anything to worry about.

The entrance gate was a few yards ahead. She slowed her pace as she drew closer. Millie didn't recognize the man guarding the gate. "Where is Brody?"

"He no work tonight," the man said. "They send him back to his cabin. He be back tomorrow."

Millie thanked the man before she turned on her heel and hurried toward the safety of the ship. At least she wouldn't have to worry about her friend for one night.

Deep in her own thoughts, Millie was caught off guard as a man emerged from the shadows, reached out and clamped onto her arm in an ironclad grip.

"What are you doing here?"

***

Millie's first instinct was to scream at the top of her lungs. Instead, she jerked her arm with all her might, pulling her attacker into the light. It was Dave Patterson.

"You scared me half to death," Millie gasped. "What are you doing out here, lurking in dark shadows?"

"I came out to send Brody back to his cabin to rest and then figured I'd do a little undercover surveillance since I was already here."

"I noticed Brody out here earlier and thought I'd check on him," Millie said.

"You shouldn't be wandering outside alone after dark, even if you are inside the gate," Patterson said.

"You're right," Millie agreed. "I wasn't thinking."

Patterson snorted.

"Were you able to figure out who left the threatening note in Brody's door?"

"I asked Brody and he said he has no idea. He has no idea why he's being targeted or why he was attacked. He swears he saw someone lying in the corridor yet we can't find a record of any employee who was hurt. I'm at a loss."

Millie had a dark, terrible thought. "What about missing employees?"

"I already looked into that," Patterson said. "We had a couple crewmembers who left the ship after we docked in Miami. They haven't returned or showed up for their shift but that's not unusual. Crewmembers grow weary of working long hours and they just walk off the job."

"But no one has been reported missing?" Millie probed.

"No."

Millie thought about Sharky and the maintenance crew. She wondered if Patterson knew of Sharky, started to say something and then changed her mind. She wanted to speak to Sharky first, believing she would have better luck getting him to talk than if the head of security showed up on his doorstep.

Patterson placed a light hand on her arm. "I'll walk you back to the ship." Millie hated to admit it, but she was relieved Patterson was there.

She silently vowed if she ventured out again after dark she would bring someone with her, and bring her Taser. "I hear you're filling in for Andy next week while he heads home."

"Don't remind me," Millie groaned. "I have no idea how he talked me into taking over for him."

"You don't give yourself enough credit, Millie."

Millie still wasn't convinced it would be 'smooth sailing.' Even with Andy at the helm, there always seemed to be at least one crisis. She remembered an incident, only a couple months earlier during the 'Gem of the Seas' show.

The headliner, a singer, was in the middle of her solo song. A set of cables, attached to a belt around her waist, began to lift her off the stage, giving her the appearance of floating in air. Halfway up, the cables jammed and she stopped abruptly, dangling in midair.

The staff quickly closed the curtains and ended the show. It took a good 45 minutes before they were able to fix the cable motor, and guide the harness ropes and terrified performer to safety.

It was this type of sticky situation Millie feared the most, but it was too late now. She had committed to filling in for Andy and there was no way she would change her mind. It was a sink or swim situation and she resolved not to fret over things that had not yet happened.

Millie yawned and quickly covered her mouth. It had been a long day and tomorrow promised to be even longer. She thanked Patterson for accompanying her back to the ship and they parted ways in the atrium.

The cabin was dark and quiet when Millie stepped inside. After slipping into her pajamas, washing her face and brushing her teeth, she climbed into bed.

Siren of the Seas had recently given the crew the option of installing custom curtains, which ran the length of the bunks. They were thick, room darkening curtains, perfect for blocking out light. They even managed to muffle some of the cabin noise.

Millie pulled the curtain shut before flipping her bunkbed light off and snuggling under the covers. She prayed for Brody's safety and then added her nightly prayer that Nic and she would be able to marry and live aboard the ship as husband and wife.

When she finished praying for her family, Millie flipped onto her side and promptly fell asleep.

Sometime during the night, Millie heard Danielle stumble into the cabin and creep into the bathroom. She dozed off but woke to a strange sound.

Millie bolted upright in bed when she realized it was the sound of Danielle vomiting in the bathroom. She quickly flipped the light on and flung the bunk curtain aside as she sprang from her bed.

"Danielle! Are you all right?" Millie whispered through the bathroom door. She could've sworn she heard a low moan so she eased the door open.

Danielle was sitting on the bathroom floor, her arms wrapped around the sides of the toilet and her head hanging over the top.

Millie dropped to her knees. "Oh my gosh."

"I feel terrible," Danielle whispered right before she threw up. Her long blonde locks fell forward and the tips almost touched the inside of the toilet bowl.

Millie grabbed a ponytail holder from the counter and quickly pulled Danielle's hair back to keep it out of the way.

Next, Millie wet a washcloth with cool water and pressed it to Danielle's forehead.

"I feel awful." Danielle scooched forward and leaned her shoulder against the wall.

"What happened? Were you partying too much?" Danielle wasn't much of a party girl. Millie could count on one hand the number of times she'd seen Danielle drink alcohol.

"No. I was hanging out with some of the bartenders and dancers drinking Sprite of all things. Next thing I know, I started to feel woozy, like I was going to pass out so I hurried back here."

"Someone spiked your Sprite?" Millie had heard of date rape drugs being slipped into unsuspecting women's drinks but she'd never heard of it on board Siren of the Seas.

"Let me get some water." She tiptoed over Danielle and hurried to the small refrigerator where she reached inside, grabbed a bottled water and carried it to the bathroom. Millie unscrewed the top and handed it to the young woman.

"Thanks." Danielle downed half the bottle. "I'm feeling better already."

"Did you leave your Sprite on the counter and use the restroom?"

"Yeah, dumb me. When I came back, the group I was hanging out with had left and there were two other crewmembers I didn't recognize sitting at the bar. They were acting a little weird so I grabbed my drink and headed to the other side of the bar where Sarah and Nikki were playing pool. When I looked back, the guys at the bar were staring at me. Something told me not to drink my Sprite but I ignored my gut instinct and guzzled half the glass. When I started to feel a little woozy, I left the drink on the table and hurried home."

Danielle struggled to her feet, swaying to the side as she attempted to maneuver around the toilet. "I still feel a little sick to my stomach. I think I better go to bed."

Millie stayed with her while she rinsed her mouth and brushed her teeth. Danielle didn't bother undressing and Millie insisted she take the bottom bunk so that she'd be closer to the bathroom.

After Millie settled Danielle in the lower bunk, she pulled the curtain halfway and climbed into the top bunk. "Just holler if you need anything, Danielle."

"Thanks Millie/Mom," Danielle said. "Millie to the rescue again."

Millie shut the light off and closed her eyes but it was a long time before she was finally able to fall asleep. She was determined to have Danielle file a report in the morning.

Danielle was still sleeping when Millie climbed down from the bunk the next morning. She quietly tiptoed to the bathroom to get ready.

By the time she emerged, a bleary-eyed Danielle was sitting on the edge of the bunk.

"How are you feeling?"

"Like I got hit by a semi-truck." Danielle eased off the bed and shuffled to the bathroom.

Millie could hear her banging around inside. When Danielle stepped out of the bathroom, she was dressed and looked a hundred percent better. "I feel better already."

"You should try to eat something," Millie said. "Maybe some dry toast or a bagel."

The crew dining room was deader than a doornail and the women had the place to themselves. Millie insisted Danielle sit down while she filled a tray with food she hoped her young friend could eat. She carried the food and a cup of coffee and juice to the table.

"After you finish eating, we're going to Dave Patterson's office to tell him what happened." Millie placed the food and coffee in front of Danielle and propped the empty tray next to her chair.

Danielle bit the corner of her dry wheat toast. "What if I just had a bug or ate something bad?"

"Do you think that's the case Danielle?"

"No. I think someone slipped something into my drink."

"Then you need to report it. You may be able to save someone else from becoming a victim."

"You're right," Danielle agreed. After they finished eating, they trekked down the I-95 corridor to the other end and Dave Patterson's office.

Thankfully, he was in his office and motioned them inside. "What's with the serious expressions? Don't tell me you wandered off the ship again last night and got into trouble."

"No." Millie shook her head. "Danielle has something to tell you."

Danielle cast Millie an uneasy glance before she sucked in a breath. "I think someone in the employee lounge slipped a drug in my drink last night."

Patterson's jaw tightened. "A date rape drug?"

"Yes." Danielle told Patterson exactly what she'd told Millie and ended the story with Millie insisting she file a report.

"Danielle is not a drinker," Millie said. "When she came home last night, she was sicker than a dog."

"Did you get a good look at the men who were sitting at the bar when you returned from the bathroom?"

Danielle shook her head. "No. It was dark and to be honest, I wasn't paying much attention. I can tell you they didn't look familiar." She paused. "Now that I think about it, it was right around eleven o'clock because Dario, one of the regular bartenders, had just left. He said he was heading back to the cabin to catch the eleven o'clock local news.

"Do you know who was working the employee bar last night after Dario left?" Patterson asked. "Never mind. I can find out." He reached inside his side drawer, pulled out a manila file folder, opened it up and reached for the paper on top.

Danielle and Millie sat in silence while Patterson filled out the report. He set the pen on top of the paper and slid them across the desk. "Take a look to make sure I didn't miss anything."

Danielle lifted the sheet of paper and studied the front. "Yes. This sums it up."

"Sign and date the bottom."

After Danielle signed, she slid the papers across the desk and clutched her stomach. "I think my toast is planning a revolt."

Millie stood. "I'll walk with you to the cabin." She waited until Danielle was in bed before slipping out of the cabin and heading upstairs to track down Annette.

It was time to pay Sharky a visit.

Chapter 9

Clang...lang.

"Are you sure we're going the right way?" Millie shifted her gaze and glanced nervously at the large metal pipes overhead that were rattling to beat the band. It sounded as if they were going to burst at any moment, spraying her with who knew what.

"Yeah," Annette said. "I'm a hundred percent sure. Now you know why Frank Bauer is content to let someone else supervise this area of the ship." She sniffed the air. "You smell that?"

The stench of something rotting hung heavy in the air.

Millie wrinkled her nose. "It smells putrid, like rotting produce or worse."

"We're close now." Annette pointed at the double set of swinging doors a short distance away.

Lining one side of the corridor were empty luggage carts. On the other side of the corridor stacked floor-to-ceiling, were empty wooden pallets.

The women pushed the swinging doors open and loud voices filled the hall. Bright light illuminated the corridor and as they drew closer, Millie could see an open cargo door with a ramp leading to the dock.

Millie darted to the side as a forklift raced up the ramp and careened around the corner.

"Watch where you're going!" Annette yelled at the driver, who gave her the middle finger before speeding full steam ahead down the long corridor.

Annette's reprimand drew the attention of several of the workers. One of them, who had been stacking boxes of floor tiles, made his way over. "You two shouldn't be down here. It's dangerous. The crew exit is two decks up."

"Now you warn us," Millie muttered. "We're looking for Sharky."

"Who's looking for Sharky?"

"We are." Annette pointed at Millie. "Is there a problem with that?"

The man shrugged. "I don't have a problem with it but Sharky might." He tipped his head to a smaller corridor. "Last time I saw Sharky, he was down near the recycle bins."

"Thanks." Annette walked across the corridor and Millie hurried behind her.

"I hope we don't end up in the bin."

"You worry too much," Annette said. "What's the worst that can happen? Sharky tells us to get lost?"

Millie could think of a hundred other things that could happen. She shoved the thought aside as they entered the second corridor. Thankfully, this one wasn't nearly as congested as the one they'd just left.

The corridor was a maze of twists and turns. Unmarked metal doors lined the corridor. A sense of foreboding filled Millie as they zigzagged around another corner and the corridor narrowed again. "I'm pretty sure this is the deck where they lock up the unruly crew for punishment."

Annette grinned. "Yeah and I'm sure they only give them bread and water and chain them to rattling pipes," she teased.

"It's not funny," Millie said.

The corridor took a sharp turn and Millie came to a screeching halt when she nearly collided head-on with a man riding a black scooter, racing toward them from the opposite direction.

The first thing Millie noticed was his hair, or more precisely the style. Both sides of his head were shaved. The top of his dark brown 'do' spiked straight up and traveled forward at an angle in a Mohawk.

Millie wondered if the spikes had ever poked someone's eye out.

"We don't allow visitors down here," the man growled.

"We're looking for Sharky," Annette said.

"Who is looking for Sharky?"

Millie resisted the urge to roll her eyes. It was a déjà vu moment. "The Queen of England," she snapped.

Annette took a step forward. "Do you like to eat?"

"Of course I do. That's a stupid question."

"Good because I'm looking for Sharky and I'm the director of food and beverage."

"Well, why didn't you say so?" The man, all three feet tall of him, hopped off the scooter. He bent forward in an exaggerated bow. "Sharky Kiveski at your service."

Millie clamped a hand across her mouth to keep from laughing. Sharky was as wide as he was tall. *This guy was in charge of the night crew?*

"How may I be of assistance?"

"We heard there was an incident down here the other night and the head of night security was attacked," Annette said. "We're wondering what you know about it."

Sharky frowned. "You gonna bust my chops, too? I already told the head of security what I know. End of story."

"It's not the end of the story," Millie said. "Brody, the security guard who was attacked, was threatened again yesterday."

"We're trying to figure out who is targeting Brody and why," Annette added. "One of the maintenance guys upstairs said you might be able to shed some light on the subject."

Sharky hooked his thumbs in his pants pockets and studied Annette. "Why do you care?"

"Because he's our friend," Millie said. "We're certain he's still on someone's hit list."

"What's in it for me?"

Annette crossed her arms and stared down at Sharky. "Let's cut to the chase. What do you want? Chicken wings? A nice juicy ribeye steak with all the fixin's? My famous *Death by Chocolate* cake?"

Sharky smacked his lips as he rubbed his hands together. "Now you're talking." He tipped his head and stared at the pipes on the ceiling. "Yeah. A nice juicy medium well bone-in ribeye, baked potato loaded, don't skimp on the bacon bits and sour cream, corn on the cob with extra butter and for dessert, a nice big slice of lemon meringue pie."

Annette glanced at her watch. "It's gonna take some time to pull the meal together."

"I got plenty of time." Sharky hopped onto his scooter.

Millie noticed a set of red flames painted along the side of the scooter. Etched inside the flames was the word *Sharky*.

"My dinner break isn't until six. I'll work on a little more intel for you two gals before our next meeting."

"We'll be back at six sharp," Annette promised. "How will we know where to find you?"

"Meet me in my office," Sharky said. "When you reach the main corridor, make a right. My office is the second door on the right. You can't miss it. My name is on the front."

"Sharky?"

"Yeah. It stands for Supervisor of Human Administration Representing Keel Yeoman."

Annette frowned.

"You know, the keel runs along the centerline of the ship and Yeoman is a petty naval officer. Yeoman is a stretch but it's the only word that fit my acronym."

The title was bigger than Sharky was. "I thought it had to do with your 'do'." Annette pointed at Sharky's Mohawk and then patted the top of her head.

"This?" Sharky ran the palm of his hand over the spikes. "No. This is just for looks. The chicks dig it."

"We'll take your word for it," Annette said. "See you at six."

Sharky lifted his hand in mock salute before flipping the switch on the scooter. It let out a loud *popping noise* as it backfired, scaring Millie half to death.

Sharky snickered at her before twisting the throttle, popping a wheelie and zipping around the corner and out of sight.

Millie waited until he was gone before speaking. "What if he's just blowing smoke and doesn't know squat?"

"There's always the possibility," Annette said. "Nothing ventured, nothing gained. All it's gonna take is a little work on my part to fix his meal. You never know, Sharky might not be a wealth of information this time, but having someone on the inside at this level could prove helpful down the road."

"Good point."

"Always gotta be thinkin' ahead." Annette tapped the side of her forehead. "It doesn't hurt to have friends in low places, just like the country song."

"Literally," Millie laughed.

The women retraced their steps and trudged up the steps to the land of the living. Millie hoped Sharky would be able to provide some sort of useful information. If not, Brody was scheduled to work the night shift that evening and her gut told her something bad was going to happen if they couldn't figure out who had it in for their friend.

Annette headed upstairs to check on the dinner menu and prep for Sharky's steak dinner while Millie made her way to Brody's cabin to chat with him.

There was a *Do Not Disturb* sign hanging from the doorknob and not wanting to disturb his rest, she retraced her steps.

Her next stop was to check on Danielle. The cabin was empty and Millie's bed was made. Relieved that Danielle was feeling better, it was time to return to the library to work on her inventory.

While she worked, she mulled over Brody's situation. Maybe Sharky did know more than he let on and he was just milking it for a free meal. Heaven knew some of the unidentifiable dishes inside the crew-dining hall left a lot to be desired.

Millie couldn't blame him for trying to get a decent meal out of the deal. She wondered if the crew resented Brody's move up the ladder and if they resented staff like her who were allowed special privileges that they weren't.

She'd never heard a negative comment but then again, many of them knew of her relationship with Captain Armati so there was a good chance they wouldn't reveal how they really felt.

This led Millie to wonder if her friends were really friends or if they just sucked up to her because of who she was. She hoped not.

There was also the body Brody swore he saw. Millie hoped to be able to talk to Brody, to see if he could remember anything else. The fact that Patterson admitted there was a small puddle of blood near Brody but it wasn't his, was suspect.

By lunchtime, Millie was three quarters of the way finished with inventorying the books. She'd had to toss out a couple of them. One was missing several pages while another appeared to have been used as a child's coloring book. A bunch of the pages were decorated with crayon marks.

It was a shame since the hardcover book was a new release.

She wandered to the buffet area only to discover it was closed and the *Waves* renovation project was in full swing. The ship's crew had moved the tables and chairs to the back deck, and several workers were on their hands and knees, chipping away at the old tile floors.

She headed to the lido buffet and grabbed a plate full of food. Millie carried the food, along with a glass of tea back to the library and settled in at the window seat overlooking the bay.

It was a gorgeous Florida afternoon. Millie munched on her hotdog as she watched fishing boats and jet skis sail down the open waterway.

A Coast Guard vessel cruised back and forth and Millie wondered if the Coast Guard was guarding the ship.

She finished her food and placed the dirty plate off to the side before resuming her task of inventory. The thrill of the project wore off and grew tedious as the afternoon wore on. Finally, by late afternoon, she finished the inventory and exited the library.

Millie dropped her dirty dishes in the kitchen, hoping to chat with Annette but she was nowhere in sight so she headed downstairs and made a last minute detour to Brody's cabin. The *Do Not Disturb* sign was gone so Millie tapped on the door.

It opened a crack and Millie caught a glimpse of Brody peeking through the opening. When he spotted Millie, he opened the door. "I heard you were looking for me."

"I'm worried about you, Brody," Millie said.

In the bright hall light, she was able to get a good look at Brody. He looked okay, except for a large angry mark on the back of his head.

"I might as well invite you in since I know you won't let up until you're sure I'm okay." Brody opened the door and limped across the room.

"Sorry if I'm moving slow. I twisted my ankle during my fall."

Brody's cabin sported the same layout as Millie and Danielle's, minus the desk chair, which was missing. In its place was a cooler. She gingerly sat on top of the cooler.

"I'm concerned about you, Brody," Millie said. "I'm sure you heard about the note I found tucked in your door. This isn't over."

Brody sat on the edge of the lower bunk and propped his elbows on his knees. "Something's not right. Right before I was attacked, I heard some grunting noises and a loud thump. When I rounded the corner of the back corridor, I saw someone lying on the corridor floor."

"One thing we know for certain, your attacker is still on the loose," Millie said. "Not to mention the note."

Brody waved his hand dismissively. "Someone is trying to scare me off and Brody Rourke don't scare easy. They caught me off guard last time but it won't happen again." He pounded his chest. "We ex-marines are tough as nails."

Alarmed by Brody's lack of concern over his safety, Millie switched tactics. She remembered how Marcus had mentioned the last port stop in San Juan.

"You didn't get into it with the night maintenance crew at all, no harsh words, no warnings, nothing..." Millie's voice trailed off.

"Like I said, I ain't gonna worry about it." Brody stood. "I got a job to do and short of them taking me out permanently, that's exactly what I plan to do."

This was exactly what Millie was afraid of.

Chapter 10

It was close to Sharky's dinner hour and Millie arrived in the galley early to see if Annette needed help.

She found her friend rummaging around in the fridge. Annette pulled the lemon meringue pie from the cooler and reached inside the drawer for a knife. "Brody swears he heard noises and thumping and saw a body?"

"Yeah," Millie said. "He plans to show up for his shift, starting at eleven tonight and I have a feeling he's walking right into a trap."

Annette finished working on the crewmember's Mexican themed dinner. She barked out instructions to her staff in the galley and then threw Sharky's steak on the grill while Millie scrubbed a potato, stabbed it a few times and stuck it in the microwave.

"Where's the corn on the cob?"

"We don't have any." Annette looked up from the grill. "He's gonna have to settle for fresh frozen sweet corn. It's in the freezer to the right."

Millie grabbed the sweet corn and filled a glass bowl. While Annette grilled the steak, Millie finished cooking the baked potato and warmed the dish of corn.

Annette flipped the steak over. "Perfect." She plated the steak while Millie added the potato to the side and ladled a large spoonful of corn in the open space.

When the dish was covered, Annette carried that while Millie followed behind, carrying the lemon meringue pie. "I always heard the way to a man's heart was through his stomach."

"Me too," Millie said. "It never worked with Roger. He hated my cooking."

Annette stopped abruptly. "Are you a terrible cook?"

"I don't think so, at least my kids never complained." Looking back on their thirty plus years of marriage, Roger had complained a lot. He nitpicked her housekeeping, her bookkeeping and how she disciplined their two children, Beth and Blake.

Nic, so far, was the complete opposite. He didn't seem at all interested in whether she could cook or clean. He'd never asked about her personal finances, although she told him she'd gotten the house on Reed's Lake as part of the divorce settlement. In exchange, she'd signed off her rights to *Central Michigan Private Investigators,* the company Roger and she had started during the early years of their marriage.

As part of the settlement, she'd also gotten a couple of retirement accounts. The material and monetary possessions had been split almost evenly. Because of some recent investments she'd made, Millie would live comfortably in her later years.

Since her room, board and all meals were part of her work package, she'd saved almost every penny she made as assistant cruise director. She planned to hang onto the extra money as a safety cushion.

Now that she thought about it, she had no idea what kind of financial shape Nic was in. It was something they needed to talk about. What if he was broke? She quickly dismissed the thought. Surely, a ship's captain made good money, and like her, he didn't need to spend his income on housing, food or even utilities.

"Earth to Millie." Annette snapped her fingers in Millie's face.

"Sorry. I got a little mentally sidetracked."

The women continued their descent down the steps to the lowest level of the ship. The smell of something decaying or rotting was even stronger than it had been earlier and Millie gasped. "That's a terrible odor."

"I agree," Annette said. "I'm not sure I want to know what's causing it."

They picked up the pace as they hurried down the corridor, passing by several workers who were painting yellow safety stripes along each side of the corridor.

They stopped in front of the door marked *SHARKY*.

"I guess this is it." Annette shifted the covered plate to her other hand and rapped on the door before reaching for the knob.

She opened the door and stuck her head around the corner.

Millie followed her inside and almost burst out laughing. Sharky was sitting behind the desk with his feet propped on top. He was leaning so far back that the tips of his spiked hair touched the wall behind him.

He glanced at the clock on the wall. "I thought you weren't going to show."

Sharky pulled his legs off the desk and scooched in as he rubbed his hands together and eyed the dishes Annette and Millie were carrying. "I've been thinkin' about my big juicy steak all day."

Annette lifted the cover and waved it over the plate. The tantalizing aroma of grilled meat filled the air. "I picked one of the choicest pieces, just for you, Sharky. There's also a loaded baked potato with extra bacon bits, scallion, melted cheese, butter and lots of sour cream."

He studied the plate. "I don't see my corn on the cob."

"We don't have any," Annette said. "As in, not a single piece on the ship."

"But it was part of the deal." Sharky began to pout.

Annette replaced the lid, covering the steak. "We can take the food back to the kitchen and call off our deal."

"No. No. Corn is corn, I guess."

"That's what I thought," Annette said.

Millie held out the large piece of lemon meringue pie. "And I have dessert. I tasted it myself and it's delicious."

Sharky reached for the tray and Millie jerked back. "Not so fast. We have a deal."

"I got so distracted by the food, I almost forgot. Listen, I don't know much about the ins and outs but here's what I do know." Sharky motioned for them to have a seat.

Millie was convinced it was more that Sharky wanted to keep a close eye on the food than to be hospitable.

Millie set the pie on the desk but kept a firm grip on the plate.

Annette eased into the seat next to her. "We're all ears."

"Last week during our port stop in San Juan, a bunch of my night crew decided to head into the red light district for a little fun. Good thing they didn't tell me ahead of time or I woulda knocked a few heads together."

Millie interrupted. "Red light district?"

"It's where the 'ladies of the night' hang out. There are usually bars and pubs of ill repute in these areas," Annette said. "I've heard of it. San Juan's red light area is on the edge of the historic district."

"Right," Sharky agreed. "I mean, I don't know for certain, but that's what I heard. Anyway, a few of my guys were biding their time in one of the…" Sharky raised his hands and made quotation marks with his fingers. "…clubs. They were on their way back when they recognized Brody. He was walkin' into a bar across the street from the one they were leaving."

"Brody was hooking up with a hooker?" Millie was surprised. Brody was a nice looking young man. She found it hard to believe he had to "buy" a woman's time.

"Not quite." Sharky shook his head. "He was goin' into the Emerald Isle Club."

It was beginning to dawn on Millie where Sharky was headed. Annette must have been on the same wavelength. "Let me guess. It's a gay bar."

"Bingo."

Millie slouched in her chair, her mind swirling. "I had no idea."

"A couple of my guys started complain' sayin' his type is infiltrating the night shift. When I questioned them about Brody's attack, they swear they had nuttin' to do with it and I believe them. End of story."

Sharky lunged forward and snatched the plate of food from Annette's grip. "Now can I eat?" He didn't wait for her to answer as he removed the cover and reached for the dinner roll. Sharky took a big bite and chewed noisily. "I hope you brought some silverware."

Annette reached inside her apron pocket and pulled out a set of wrapped silverware. "It's not the end of the story because someone stuck a threatening note in Brody's door."

Sharky belched loudly. "They're a tough bunch, the crew down here but like I said, they swore they had nothing to do with Brody's attack." He sawed off a large chunk of steak and shoved it in his mouth as he rolled his eyes. "I could die happy right now."

"I take it you like the food," Annette teased.

Sharky glanced at Annette. "This is so good. I'd ask you to marry me if I wasn't already married."

"Be still my beating heart."

They watched as Sharky inhaled the rest of the food on his plate and reached for the piece of pie. "I shoulda asked for a couple pieces of fried chicken too." He eyed Annette. "Anything else you need to know?"

"No." Annette stood. "We appreciate the information."

Sharky looked up from the dessert dish. "Anytime."

"Annette." Annette pointed to Millie. "She's Millie."

"Got it. Millie and Annette. Anytime I can trade a gourmet dinner for a little info. Count me in. I got more dirt on Siren of the Seas' crew than the captain does."

Millie snorted and Annette gave her a warning glance. The less their new best bud, Sharky, knew about them, the better.

"We'll be sure to keep you in mind," Annette assured him before they made their way out of Sharky's office.

After Annette closed the door, she looked around to make sure they were alone. "I think we should keep this between the two of us."

Millie nodded. "I couldn't agree more. If Brody wants people to know the details of his personal life, I'm sure he'll let us know."

Keeping one's personal life personal while working on board a cruise ship was a daunting task but Millie vowed to keep Brody's secret. It was none of her business, or anyone else's business for that matter.

"So now what?" Annette asked.

"Brody plans to work the night shift, guarding the ship's security gate outside," Millie said. "I think I'm gonna hang out on the promenade deck, at least for a little while, to keep an eye on him."

"I'll join you," Annette said. "Two sets of eyes are better than one."

Chapter 11

"They ought to add a little padding to these loungers," Millie complained as she shifted for what seemed like the hundredth time and adjusted the pool towel she'd brought with her in an attempt to add a little cushion.

So far, the stakeout of Brody's security post watch was a yawner. He'd settled in at twenty-three hundred hours or eleven p.m. An overhead security light made the task of keeping an eye on Brody a little easier. It was beaming brightly on both him and the entrance gate.

"I give someone attacking Brody a 50/50 chance," Annette said. "He's sitting in a spotlight. No one in their right mind is gonna jump him there. Thugs want to do their business in the dark when no one is looking."

Annette had a valid point. Not only that, Brody would be on guard tonight since it was his first night back to work.

Millie glanced at her watch. "Let's hang out another half an hour and if nothing happens, I'm ready to pack it in."

The time passed slowly and Millie decided they were wasting their time and precious hours, which could be better spent sleeping.

"I'm packing it in." Annette wiggled off the edge of the chair and slowly stood, lifting both hands over her head in a long stretch.

"I guess I might as well, too." Millie cast a final glance at Brody's lone figure and picked up her pool towel.

She was glad nothing had happened to Brody but deep down, she knew her young friend wasn't out of the woods yet. The fact he'd already been attacked once and then threatened again was cause for concern.

The women parted ways when they reached the crew hall but not before Millie thanked Annette for keeping her company and apologized for wasting their time.

"Ah. Don't worry about it." Annette waved dismissively. "You're a good friend Millie. I'm sure you would've done the same for me."

Millie's steps dragged as she made her way to her cabin. She slipped her keycard in the slot and eased the door open, hoping that if Danielle were in the cabin, she wouldn't wake her.

She needn't have worried. Bright lights filled the room and Danielle was lying on her bunk watching television.

Danielle set the remote next to her. "Where have you been?"

Millie grinned at the 'motherly' tone in her voice. "Keeping an eye on Brody."

"I was worried half to death. I tried calling you on the radio," she added accusingly.

Millie absentmindedly reached for her radio, still hooked to her belt. "I turned it down since I'm off duty."

Danielle sprung from the bunk, landing lightly on her feet. "Next time, leave me a note or let me know. I thought something happened to you."

Millie wasn't much of a late nighter. She was more of an early riser.

"So I take it Brody is okay?"

"Yeah." Millie shrugged out of her sweater and hung it on the hook inside her closet. "I was so sure someone was going to attack Brody again."

"I did a walk by earlier," Danielle said. "Brody was sitting in a spotlight. Not only that, he's probably on guard expecting someone to attack him again, which would be the perfect reason it won't happen."

"That's what Annette said."

"While you were wasting your time watching Brody, I was down in the crew lounge trying to see if I could figure out who slipped something in my drink the other night. I still don't have a clue but I found out another interesting tidbit of information while I was there."

Danielle continued. "A few of the regulars were playing poker and discussing Brody's attack. I figured if I hung around long enough and after they'd had a few drinks they'd start talking. You know the saying; *'loose lips sink ships', or is* it 'loose lips sink mighty ships?'"

"What did you find out?" Millie was all ears.

"They claim Brody was attacked by one of the security guys. They want him off the ship. They called him a *poof*. A poof is slang for a gay guy."

Millie remembered how Sharky had said some of the crew spotted Brody entering the Emerald Isle Club in San Juan.

It didn't make any sense. Brody had made offhand comments to Millie about finding a girlfriend, but maybe it was a cover to hide his true feelings.

"I." Millie slumped in the chair, her mind whirling. The revelation didn't change Millie's feelings toward Brody one iota. She was a firm believer in *Judge not lest you be judged*.

It wasn't up to her to either condemn or condone her friend's lifestyle. But others, she knew, would not be quite so neutral, especially a rough and rowdy bunch of maintenance or security workers.

The pieces were starting to fall into place. "It narrows down the list of attackers," Millie said sarcastically. "His cabin mate, his co-workers, any male on board the ship who is prejudiced towards gay men."

"Right," Danielle agreed.

Millie wondered if Dave Patterson had heard the gossip. It was against Majestic Cruise Line's company policy to discriminate against any employee or passenger based on race, religion, sex, age, sexual orientation, etc., but that wouldn't necessarily stop someone from trying to intimidate a co-worker they felt didn't 'fit in.'

Although the cruise ship was like a floating city, it was a lot "cozier" when you worked and lived on board.

"Now what?" Millie didn't want to confront Brody about what she'd discovered. It was none of her business. It was also no longer a secret. Sharky had heard the story. The ship's crew in the lounge was talking about it. News spread like wildfire among crew.

"That's not all," Danielle said. "The guys started to get a little wound up so Kell, the bartender on duty, called in security to settle them down and you'll never guess who showed up."

"Brody," Millie whispered. "But I saw him working the gate."

"Apparently not the first part of his shift because Brody and another of the night security came in to tell them to cool their jets."

Danielle continued. "I thought Brody was gonna get into it with Isaac. He's a big mouth and always stirring up trouble. It was him and another goon who sometimes hangs out at night playing cards. His name is Hugh. After Brody left, Isaac kept saying he was willing to bet some of his poker chips Brody would be off the ship permanently within 24 hours."

Millie's heart sank. "Meaning something is going to happen to Brody, worse than the attack." She grew silent as she went over her mental list of tasks for the next day, or technically that day since it was well past midnight.

There was no way Millie could sleep knowing Brody was in imminent danger. "I'm going down to the security office to talk to whoever is on duty. Someone needs to know what's going on."

"I'll go with you."

Millie glanced at Danielle's fitted leggings and baggy sweatshirt.

"What?" Danielle tugged on the bottom of her Miami Hurricane's sweatshirt. "I'm off duty and these clothes are comfy."

"If you say so."

The women stepped out into the hall and headed toward security, one deck up.

"Leggings are the new blue jeans." Danielle picked up the pace to keep up with Millie. "They have super cute patterns and they're inexpensive."

Millie stopped abruptly at the bottom of the stairwell. "They look adorable on you, Danielle, but you have the shape to wear them. I would look like the top side of a bumpy camel's back."

"You have a very trim shape for a woman your age," Danielle argued.

Millie frowned and started up the steps.

"I meant that as a compliment. I bet you're in better shape than most of the women your age. I remember looking at Delilah and wondering what in the world your ex was thinking, leaving you for that woman...God rest her soul." Danielle made a cross sign on her chest.

Millie grudgingly admitted she was in better shape than she'd been in years. With her aversion to elevators and the number of decks and length of the cruise ship, she'd lost a good twenty pounds since joining the cruise line.

She loved her job, her friends and was engaged to the most wonderful man in the world. God had blessed Millie in so many ways.

"I'm still not sold on leggings." Millie paused when she reached the next level. "Sweatpants maybe, leggings nope. I'm too old."

Danielle snorted. "Your birthday is coming up. Maybe the birthday genie will surprise you with a pair."

Millie could see the glow of light beaming through the frosted glass pane of the security office's door. "Good. Someone is in the office."

When they reached the door, Millie tapped lightly on the glass before opening the door and peeking around the corner. Felippe, one of the security guards, sat behind the desk.

"Millie." He waved her in. "What are you doing up this late?"

"I was wondering if Dave Patterson was around," Millie said.

Danielle followed her into the office and closed the door behind them. "We have something important to discuss with him."

"Ah. He's in his cabin sleeping but he keeps his radio on." Felippe reached for the walkie-talkie, sitting on the desk. "Would you like me to call him?"

"No." Millie shook her head. "I don't want to wake him. I guess it can wait until morning."

"Are you sure?"

"We're sure," Millie said. "What time is he scheduled to start work?"

"Eight in the morning but we're having an all-employee security meeting at 7:45 a.m. in the piano bar."

She thanked Felippe for the information and the women stepped out into the hall. "Now what?"

"We'll have to wait until morning," Millie said. "I want to run upstairs to see if Brody is still working before I turn in for the night."

"We can go together."

The upper decks were eerily quiet. It was so different from what the passenger areas were like when they were full of vacationers.

Millie headed to the railing and peered over the side.

Brody was in the same spot and Millie let out a sigh of relief. At least he was okay.

Danielle and Millie stood silently watching him for several long moments. A man wearing a yellow safety vest approached.

Brody began waving his hands back and forth.

"They're arguing," Danielle said. She had told Millie some time ago she'd studied body language.

"Too bad you don't read lips."

Danielle reached inside her back pocket, pulled out her cell phone, switched it on and snapped a picture of the two men. "I dabbled in speechreading years ago when I got into undercover work. They're too far away for me to get a read on what they're saying but based on their body language, it isn't a 'Hi, how are ya' kinda' conversation."

They stood silently observing the exchange until finally Brody slid off the stool, towering over the man.

The man turned to go.

"Good. He's leaving," Millie whispered.

The man abruptly swung back around and punched Brody in the face.

Millie watched in horror as Brody staggered from the force of the blow before regaining his footing. The man turned on his heel and stomped off while Brody, who was rubbing his jaw, watched him leave.

"Did you see that?" Danielle gasped. "The guy landed a chin check."

"Chin check?"

"Yeah. He punched him to see if he would fight back," Danielle said.

Brody was still rubbing his jaw as he climbed back on the stool.

"He could've cleaned that guy's clock," Millie said. But he didn't. He stood there, took the punch and then let the crewmember walk away.

"The guy was provoking him to fight," Danielle said. "I think I recognized him."

"Really? Who was it?" Millie asked.

"I don't want to say for sure until I take a closer look at the picture I took."

Brody's lone silhouette cast a long shadow across the dock. Millie could've sworn she saw his shoulder's slump. The unprovoked attacks had to be wearing on him.

After they got back to the cabin, Danielle and Millie studied the blurred picture Danielle had taken.

"This guy reminds me of Isaac, the jerk from the bar, but now I'm starting to doubt myself." Danielle shut the phone off and set it on the counter. "Brody is the only person who can tell us for sure who punched him."

Millie offered a silent prayer for her young friend. "I'm ready to turn in. Tomorrow is a new day and I plan to get to the bottom of these attacks if it's the last thing I do."

Chapter 12

Millie tossed and turned all night as she worried about Brody. Maybe she could convince Patterson to switch Brody to another shift until this whole thing blew over and the crew turned their attention to someone or something else.

There was also the puddle of blood Patterson noticed and Brody's insistence he'd heard noises and then seen someone lying on the corridor floor. Something wasn't adding up.

It was still early when Millie gave up on sleeping. She crawled out of her bunk and crept to the bathroom.

When she emerged, Danielle's soft snores filled the small space and Millie snuck out of the room without disturbing her.

Millie's plan was to talk to Patterson. His shift hadn't started yet so she headed to the library to get started on her board game project and mull over the list of suspects.

Perhaps Brody had recently ended a relationship and the spurned lover was trying to get Brody fired. She hadn't considered that angle.

She pulled out the Candy Land game and dumped the colored game pieces on the table. First, there was Isaac, the guy Danielle mentioned from the bar. Danielle said Brody's attacker reminded her of him. He also said Brody would be off the ship in 24 hours. Millie jotted his name on a slip of paper.

There was also the second man in the bar, Hugh something. She wrote his name next.

There was also Brody's roommate. She made a mental note to track him down. There was also Sharky. Millie suspected he knew more than he let on.

She worked on sorting board games until her grumbling stomach reminded her it was time to eat.

The kitchen crew had turned the outdoor grill area into a breakfast buffet. Millie filled her plate with food, made a beeline for the beverage machines to grab a cup of caffeine and began searching for an empty table.

Millie nearly passed by Brody, who was sitting alone at a large table. "Mind if I join you?"

Brody looked up. A small welt was forming on the cleft of his chin. She set her tray on the table before pulling out an empty chair. "Brody! What happened?"

He shook his head. "What are you talking about?"

"The bruise on your chin."

Brody gingerly touched his chin. "It's nothing. I'm fine."

Millie eased into her seat, unfolded her silverware and smoothed the napkin in her lap. Beating around the bush was getting her nowhere so she decided to take a direct approach.

"Someone who works on this ship is determined to get you fired or worse yet, continue attacking you until you quit."

"I'm not going anywhere." Brody reached for a glazed donut and took a big bite.

"At first I thought someone was jealous of your promotion but I've heard the rumors there's another reason and it has something to do with the Emerald Isle and your recent visit."

"That's a bunch of garbage," Brody said. "Besides that, it's nobody's business."

"I couldn't agree more, but unfortunately someone else thinks differently. They need to be fired." Millie sprinkled salt on her eggs and reached for her fork. "Patterson won't tolerate these attacks."

Millie decided to change tactics. "You could just let them provoke you to the point of fighting back and then Patterson will have no choice but to fire you."

"Won't happen."

"I hope you're right." Brody was stubborn as a mule and Millie could tell from the look on his face he wasn't going to help her...help him.

Brody inhaled his food and stood. "Got a meeting with Patterson." He picked up his empty plate and then reached for his dirty napkin. "Thanks for trying to help Millie. It's times like this you know who your real friends are and it looks like I only got a couple."

He didn't wait for a reply as he turned on his heel and trudged off. Brody may have been trying to convince Millie to let it go, but it had the opposite effect. It was time for the good guy to finish first and Millie vowed to make sure it happened.

***

"I need another meal to bribe Sharky."

Annette smoothed her wayward strands of hair and eased her chef's hat on her head. "Well, we could do steak and eggs since we know he likes steak."

While Annette fried a steak in the pan, Millie explained what Danielle and she had witnessed the previous evening. "I ran into Brody at breakfast. The man has dug in his heels and refuses to discuss last night's attack. Word on the ship is something is going to happen to Brody by the end of today."

"Another attack?" Annette asked.

"Danielle told me last night a crewmember in the employee lounge was bragging Brody would be off the ship by the end of the day. There were two of them - Isaac and Hugh somebody. Later, she and I headed to an upper deck to keep an eye on him. We were only there a short time before we watched someone walk over to Brody at the guard gate and punch him in the face."

Annette turned toward Millie. "Did you recognize the person?"

"Danielle thought it was the guy from the bar, Isaac, but she couldn't be certain," Millie said. "He was too far away and it was too dark to tell for sure."

She sucked in a deep breath. "I'm going to see if Sharky will let me borrow one of the night crew uniforms so I can keep an eye on Brody tonight."

"What if they don't wait until tonight? What if they go after him while he's in his cabin sleeping today?"

Millie hadn't considered that angle. "I hope not. We can't guard his room all day."

"I have a better idea. You said he's at a security meeting right now?"

"Yeah."

"Give me your access keycard and watch this steak," Annette said.

Millie removed her keycard and reluctantly placed it in Annette's outstretched hand.

"What? You don't trust me?" Annette asked.

"I do." Millie briefly closed her eyes and visions of Annette getting busted with her keycard filled her mind. "Ignorance is bliss. I'll watch Sharky's breakfast."

"Perfect." Annette darted out of the galley before Millie could change her mind.

If Annette was caught sneaking into Brody's cabin using Millie's keycard, Brody wouldn't be the only one off the ship by the end of the day.

***

Annette tucked the small audio device in her front apron pocket and slipped out of her cabin. "C187," she muttered under her breath and then smiled at a crewmember who passed her in the hall.

In and out. Annette would tuck the small device in one of the ceiling panels inside Brody Rourke's cabin and be out of there in less than 30 seconds.

She was banking on the fact the cruise lines bunked the crewmembers who worked in the same departments together, which meant if her assumption was correct, Brody's cabin mate, another member of the security crew, was also attending Patterson's mandatory meeting.

Her heart skipped a beat as she drew close to Brody's cabin. At the far end of the hall, she could see workers walking in the other direction so she passed Brody's cabin, turned around and began walking back.

The ship's crew disappeared from sight and Annette slipped Millie's keycard into the slot. She waited for the familiar beep and eased the door open. "Hello?"

No answer.

"Hello? Brody? Your door was ajar."

Still no answer.

Annette eased the door shut and then ran her hand along the wall as she searched for the light switch.

Thunk.

Following the *thunk* was a shuffling noise. Someone was inside the dark cabin with her.

Annette flipped the light on, her eyes attempting to adjust to the light. The room was empty. Convinced her mind was playing tricks on her; she inched forward and gazed into the small bathroom to her left.

Shampoo bottle samples filled the counter. Stacked in one corner were bars of unopened soap. On the other side was a pile of disposable razors. Every square inch of real estate was covered with the complimentary goodies the housekeeping staff left inside the guests' cabins.

A towering mound of dirty towels covered the floor under the sink and the stench of body odor lingered in the air.

Annette pinched her nose and breathed through her mouth as she passed the open door and hurried to the middle of the cabin. The clock was ticking and she needed to move fast.

The small desk was full of empty drink cups, dirty dishes and an array of utility grade flashlights. There was also a stack of Tasers.

Annette pulled out the first thing she laid eyes on ...a cooler, and centered it close to the side of the bunkbeds. She climbed on top and pushed on one of the ceiling tiles. A cloud of thick gray dust fell from the corner and landed squarely on her face.

The particles burned Annette's eyes and she blinked rapidly. "Ugh." She nudged the panel to the side, eased the device into the corner and then carefully slid the panel back in place, leaving only a small gap.

With a quick swipe at her face, she eased off the cooler and slid it back to its original spot.

Mission accomplished, she turned to go when the closet door flew open. "What are you doing in here?"

Chapter 13

"What am I doing in here?" Annette hissed. "What are you doing in here? Or better yet, how did you get in here?"

"Wait." Annette held up her hand. "Let's have this conversation somewhere else."

"Agreed." Danielle opened the cabin door and slipped into the hall. "Coast is clear." She waved Annette out and then let the door close behind them.

"Now. How did you get into Brody's cabin?"

"The door was ajar," Danielle said.

"For real. How did you get in there?" Annette asked.

"I just told you. I came down to talk to Brody and his door was ajar so I let myself in," Danielle insisted. "I heard the keycard in the door so I flipped the light off and hid in the closet until I realized it was you. What were you doing?"

"I slipped an audio device behind a ceiling tile so I can keep an ear out for Brody today while he's sleeping."

"But how did you get in his cabin?" Danielle asked. "I heard a keycard."

"I used a special access card."

"What?" Danielle gasped. "I can't get a special clearance card but they gave it to *you*?"

Annette started to correct her but changed her mind. "We can't all have high level security clearance."

"But you run the galley. Why would you need high-level clearance? That's not fair." Danielle stomped her foot.

"Danielle. Do you copy?" Danielle's radio began to squawk.

"Go ahead Andy."

"I need to see you in my office for a moment."

"I hope you didn't get busted," Annette teased.

"Well, if I got busted, so did you."

"True."

Danielle grumbled under her breath until the women parted ways on deck three. Annette continued climbing until she reached deck seven and then strode into the galley.

Millie, who had been pacing the floor, looked up when she spotted Annette. "Well?"

Annette reached inside her pocket and handed Millie her keycard. "It went off without a hitch until Danielle popped out of Brody's closet and scared me half to death."

"What was Danielle doing in Brody's closet?" Millie asked. "Let me guess, she was checking on Brody and his door just happened to be open and she let herself in."

"Bingo."

"So she busted you with my keycard?"

"No. I let her believe I have high level security clearance now."

"Whew." Millie rolled her eyes. "I bet that went over like gangbusters."

"Oh no. She went on and on. Poor Andy. He's going to get an earful."

"Wait until she finds out you don't have high level security clearance," Millie said. "I finished fixing Sharky's breakfast.

"Looks good. Would you like me to go with you?" Annette asked.

"No." Millie shook her head. "I gather you have some way to listen in on the audio device."

Annette pulled her cell phone from her back pocket. "Yep. I have an app. The audio comes in clear as a bell. I'll be able to hear a pin drop."

Millie thanked Annette for planting the device and then grabbed the plate of food. "Now let's see if this spectacular breakfast meal is enough to get Sharky on board for an undercover mission."

"I'm in," Annette said. "I wear a medium shirt, slacks, whatever."

"Got it. Wish me luck." Millie placed a cover on the plate of food and headed out of the galley. She passed Amit in the hall and he gave her a strange look as he eyed the plate. "Don't ask."

"Miss Millie," Amit shook his head. "I never ask any more."

"Smart man."

When Millie reached the bottom of the ship, she made a beeline for Sharky's office. The door was wide open and Sharky was leaning back in his chair, his feet propped up on the desk and an unlit cigar dangled from his mouth.

He was talking on the phone but when he caught a glimpse of Millie holding a plate of food, he quickly ended the conversation. "Gotta go. Got an important meeting to attend."

Sharky slammed the phone down "I was just thinkin' to myself, 'Sharky,' I said. 'It's time to go grab some grub'." He rubbed his hands together. "Whatcha' got?"

Millie eased the plate onto the desk. "I have steak and eggs, along with a stack of silver dollar pancakes, strips of crispy bacon, sausage links and some toast."

"Sweet. I'm beginnin' to wonder where you gals have been all my life." Sharky lunged forward to grab the dish.

"Not so fast." Millie pulled it back, out of reach. "I have a favor to ask."

"Yeah?" Sharky lifted a brow. "What kind of favor?"

"I need to borrow a couple maintenance uniforms for tonight's shift."

"You still workin' on the security guard's deal?" Sharky asked. "Heard he's leavin' after tonight."

"That's the problem," Millie said. "Someone plans to get rid of Brody and I plan to stop them."

"Fifty bucks says it's his cabin mate. He don't wanna bunk with his type."

Millie ignored the comment. The cabin mate was on the suspect list but there were others, as well. "So you'll let me borrow the uniforms?" She lifted the lid on the food.

Sharky licked his lips, his eyes never leaving the plate. "Yeah. I can spare a couple. They're in the locker in the corner."

Millie set the plate of food in front of Sharky and made her way to the metal cabinet. She rifled through the clothes until she found two pair of medium size slacks and two medium button-down shirts.

She draped them over her arm and turned to go. "What time do we report for work?"

Sharky looked up, his mouth full of food. "The second shift starts at eleven o'clock."

"We'll see you then." Millie lifted a hand to salute him before exiting the office.

"I won't be here," Sharky called out. "When you get here, ask for Reef. He's my right hand man and second in command. I'll figure something out to keep you gals busy."

Judging by the tone of Sharky's voice, she wasn't sure if that was a promise or a threat. "Reef?"

"Savage. Reef Savage."

Millie couldn't wait to find out what 'Reef' looked like. She wondered if all the maintenance supervisors had nautical nicknames. "Thanks for the heads up." She waved the pile of clothes. "Thanks for the clothes."

Sharky grunted. "I don't wanna hear nothin' about you getting into trouble down here. I got enough problems."

"We'll do our best to stay under the radar." Based on Millie's track record, she couldn't promise Sharky nothing would happen.

Thwarting an imminent attack was sure to bring some sort of confrontation.

She stopped by the gift shop to chat with Cat but the lights were off and the door locked so she headed to the kitchen. Annette, Amit and Cat were off in the corner, huddled close together.

"What." Millie was about to ask what they were doing when she spotted Annette holding her cell phone. She put a finger to her lips.

Millie jogged across the room to join them.

"...when they take you down, Bro. These dudes mean business this time."

"I can take care of myself," Brody replied. The second part of his sentence was muffled.

"I told you, no one will tell me who's been behind the attacks."

There was a loud banging noise and then silence, followed by a heavy sigh.

"That must've been Brody's cabin mate," Cat whispered.

Millie's stomach churned. "He was trying to warn Brody." She began to pace back and forth. It was frustrating Millie to no end, like knowing you were about to crash and burn and could do nothing to stop it.

"If we could just convince Brody to switch shifts until this whole thing blows over."

"He's stubborn as a mule," Millie said. "I've already tried talking to him."

"We're going blindly into this surveillance," Annette pointed out. "We have no idea who or what we're looking for. In other words, we don't have any suspects."

"Au contraire." Millie lifted an index finger. "First there's Brody's cabin mate. We also have Isaac, the big mouth in the bar. I wouldn't rule out Sharky or the night supervisor, either."

"You got the goods?" Annette pointed to the pile of clothes Millie was holding.

"Yeah. Everything is a go. We're to report downstairs at eleven sharp and ask for Reef."

Annette raised a brow. "Reef?"

"Reef Savage," Amit piped up. "His nickname is sparkplug."

"I thought Reef was his nickname." Millie was confused.

"No. Reef is his real name. Sparkplug his nickname. He a real jerk."

Great. The last thing Millie needed was to have to try to keep Brody safe, all the while having to deal with a pseudo jerk boss. At least it was only for one night. On the bright side, it would make her appreciate Andy even more.

"We'll deal with him when the time comes," Annette said. "The brunch crowd is calling and it's time for me to get back to work."

Millie placed Annette's "uniform" in the side drawer and followed Cat into the hall. "I'm free after eight tonight. Is there anything I can do to help you?" Cat asked.

"I'm sure there is. Give me a minute." Whether it was coincidence or subconscious design, most of the sleuthing, spying and undercover work was team Millie/Annette...and Danielle, but not by choice. Somehow, Danielle always managed to nose her way into Millie's investigations.

Millie rarely asked Cat to join them, but in Millie's defense, Cat had been dealing with her own issues. Now that Cat was emotionally stable, maybe it was time to include her in their mini missions.

It wouldn't hurt to have someone nearby to keep a lookout during their operation. The last thing they needed was to run into Dave Patterson or one of the other security supervisors.

Patterson hadn't specifically warned Millie to leave Brody alone but she knew he wouldn't appreciate her meddling in his affairs, especially when it involved one of his employees.

"Do you think you can handle being our lookout in case Patterson or someone else decides to check on Brody?"

"Absolutely." Cat beamed. "Tell me when and where and I'll be there."

"Thanks Cat." Millie put a light arm around her friend's shoulder as they strolled down the corridor. "Now, I have one little favor to ask."

"Sure. What's that?"

"I need to take a look at your database and track down this 'Isaac' fellow. I think it's time for us to have a chat." Millie remembered Danielle mentioning the other guy in the employee lounge the previous night when Isaac said he bet Brody would be off the ship in 24 hours.

"There's also 'Hugh' someone."

Cat fished her key from her pocket and unlocked the door to the store. Millie followed her in and to the computer in the back.

Cat turned the computer on and swiped her card before entering her access code. "Donovan is updating our database. Last time I tried to access employee information, I couldn't get in."

She slipped her reading glasses on and peered at the screen. "Ah. It's up again. What were the crewmembers' names?"

"Isaac and Hugh."

"There are too many Isaacs. I'll need a last name. Let's try searching for Hugh." Cat tapped the keyboard with the tips of her nails. "It's Hugh Mufti. He works the swing shift in maintenance."

"Meaning?" Millie asked.

"He works both night and day shift." Cat squinted her eyes. "He swiped his card at 11:41 this morning, coming back on board the ship."

"You can see what time he clocked back in?"

"Yeah. It's one of the new features Donovan installed. Kind of scary that the ship's officers are now able to track employee movements with the swipe of their card. From what I can tell, it's only in the common areas, though."

"Interesting. Big brother is watching." Millie glanced at her watch. "It's just after noon now so that means Hugh is awake."

"Yep." Cat nodded. "You wanna see what he looks like?"

"Sure." Millie hurried around the side of the counter and peered over Cat's shoulder.

Hugh's short black hair was slicked back. His eyebrows were thick and bushy and he wasn't smiling. "He looks unhappy."

"Yeah, like he didn't want his picture taken." Millie closed her eyes and attempted to burn the image of Hugh in her head.

"I have an idea. Let me try something else," Cat said as she focused her attention on the screen. "There's an Isaac Risang who purchased some drinks in the employee lounge last night. He might be the Isaac that Danielle mentioned. Here's his mugshot."

Millie studied Isaac Risang's picture. He didn't look menacing, like he would punch another person unprovoked.

"That's odd." Cat frowned.

"What's odd?"

"It looks like Isaac's records are missing."

Chapter 14

"Whoops. I take that back. They're just in a different spot." Cat reached for the mouse and scrolled to the bottom of the screen. "Isaac's cabin is C351."

"Thanks Cat. You're the bomb." Millie patted her shoulder and turned to go. "Can you look up Brody's cabin and tell me his cabin mate's name?"

"Sure." Cat's eyes narrowed. "It's Nevlin Cooper. It looks like he's only been on Siren of the Seas a couple months."

"Isaac Risang, Nevlin Cooper, Hugh Mufti." Millie repeated the names. "What about Nevlin Cooper? Any way you can bring up his profile to get a visual on him?"

"Of course." Cat tapped the keys and reached for the mouse. "Interesting. He's got a log list like a rap sheet. This dude is everywhere. Check it out." She shifted to the side and Millie leaned forward for a closer look.

The screen was filled with times and ship locations, including the main gangway and the maintenance exit area. He was also a regular at the specialty coffee bar on deck seven. "Nevlin bought several cheap drinks in the crew lounge late yesterday afternoon. An hour after his last drink purchase, he exited the main gangway."

"His last log shows he's on the ship," Cat said.

"So he may be working tonight, too," Millie said. "Is there a photo id with his information?"

"There should be." Cat continued scrolling the screen. "Here we go."

Although the picture was only a head shot, Millie immediately guessed, judging by his hollow cheekbones, the man was thin. She lowered her gaze. "Nevlin Cooper, 24 years old. 6'2", 165 lbs. Gray eyes."

She straightened her back. "I had no idea all of this personal stuff was online." Millie wondered what her online profile looked like. Maybe she didn't want to know.

"From what I've seen, it's not everyone," Cat said. She exited the screen and shut the computer off. "Like I said, Donovan just had the systems updated. None of this information was available before. I don't think we're supposed to be able to access it and I'm thinking maybe Donovan doesn't know it's out there for all to see."

"Are you gonna tell him?" Millie asked.

"I could but then he'll know I was snooping around," Cat said. "Maybe I'll just drop a hint, casually mention I saw something I shouldn't have."

She had a point. "So while we're out tonight, we need to keep an eye out for Nevlin Cooper, another security guard and Hugh Muf-something who works in maintenance."

"I'll write their names down." Cat scribbled on a blank sheet of paper and handed it to Millie. "When and where do you want to meet?"

"Meet us in the galley, no my cabin at 10:45."

Cat wrinkled her nose. "Are you going to change before we head downstairs? What if someone sees you leaving your cabin wearing a maintenance uniform?"

"Like Danielle? I hadn't thought of that. Yeah. That's not gonna work. We need a place to change that's close to the maintenance area." She tried to recall if she'd seen a restroom on the maintenance deck. Surely, they had locker rooms or somewhere to change...or maybe not. "We'll have to wing it. Meet us on deck zero, forward at 10:50."

"Got it." Cat gave a thumbs up and grinned. "If anyone can keep Brody out of trouble, it will be you."

"Or just the opposite," Millie groaned.

Cat and Millie strode out of the store. "See you later." Cat waved good-bye and sauntered off toward the bank of elevators.

Millie stood in the hallway, torn on what she should do. Part of her wanted to track down Isaac, Hugh and Nevlin, to demand that they tell her what they knew about Brody's imminent attack but if they were in on it, she didn't want to tip her hand.

What she needed to do was get some work done before Andy cornered her and asked what she'd been up to. She still needed to finish sorting through the board games and since the library was not far from the gift shop, she opted to work, which was what they were paying her for, she reminded herself.

Millie grabbed the Monopoly game first. Thankfully, the entire game was intact so she set it to the side and began sorting through the Clue game, one of her favorites.

The cards were all there but it was missing one of the weapons, the candlestick and also the brown envelope, which held the answers. She started a list of missing game pieces and after finishing, she put the game in a separate pile before moving on to Yahtzee.

As the afternoon passed, she mulled over her list of suspects. Motive and opportunity. The motive was already in place. Someone had it in for Brody. The fact the incidents occurred right after Brody visited San Juan's red light district was a clue.

He had also recently been promoted. Perhaps it had nothing to do with his visit to the Emerald Isle Club but more to do with someone who had been passed over for the promotion and now had it in for Brody.

Last but not least, perhaps Brody had stumbled on a crime in progress and there had been a body. The fact that Patterson had mentioned the blood meant he, too, wondered if Brody had seen something.

If so, what happened to that person? According to Patterson, all of the crewmembers were accounted for.

Millie thought about Hugh, who worked swing shifts in the maintenance department. Next was Nevlin, Brody's roommate. Maybe he hated Brody. It hadn't sounded like it since they'd overheard him talking to Brody, trying to warn him.

There was also Isaac, the loudmouth crewmember who said he bet Brody would be off the ship within 24 hours. That made three men who knew something.

Millie made quick work of sorting through the games and after she finished, was relieved she could finally check the library projects off her list.

After locking the library, Millie wandered aimlessly around the upper decks. The miniature golf area was in shambles as the crew worked to clear a spot for the new rock-climbing wall.

The spa area was in disarray, too. She could see several workers inside cleaning shelves and sorting through boxes of product.

Her next stop was the buffet area, which was still closed. Through the back exit door, Millie could see the tables and chairs stacked up, surrounding the pool area. Inside the restaurant, small armies of workers were cleaning the floors.

Millie backtracked to the pool area where crewmembers were filling their plates with food from the Bamboo Wok, the recently installed taco bar; as well as the grill, which was serving the usual fare of hotdogs, hamburgers and brats.

Still full from breakfast, Millie skirted the edge of the long line and bumped into someone who came up behind her.

"Fancy meeting you here."

Millie spun around, coming face-to-face with Danielle. Standing behind Danielle was Andy. "We thought we might find you up here. Let's have a power lunch."

"I'm not hungry so I'll go track down an empty table." Millie circled the deck before finding a table for four near the window, overlooking the port.

While Danielle and Andy ate, Millie gave Andy a progress report and since Millie was almost finished with the tasks on her list, Andy added a couple more, which included researching new trivia games.

Andy bit the end of his taco and reached for his napkin. "I also want to come up with some new indoor pool games. The workers are installing a retractable roof over the adults-only pool area. Since one of the biggest passenger complaints is lack of things to do during inclement weather, this would be the perfect spot to come up with some fun stuff to do indoors."

"Limbo?" Danielle asked.

"Also known as throw your back out," Millie joked.

"I like it," Andy said.

"I have another idea. We can take out the belly flop or hairy chest contest and add a male hot body contest," Danielle joked.

"Sounds kind of risqué, Danielle," Andy said. "I was thinking something a little tamer and along the lines of a contest game like *Ship Shape Pool Play*."

"What's that?"

"It's a 'Simon Says' type of game to test passenger's knowledge of shipboard terms."

"Oh, I get it. You tell them instead of 'Simon Says,' it's 'The Captain Says' move starboard and whoever gets it wrong is eliminated from the game," Millie said.

"I would definitely lose at that game," Danielle muttered.

"You're right, Danielle," Andy said, "which is why I'm putting you in charge of doing a test run with some of the other staff."

He turned to Millie. "You're up on your nautical knowledge. Make a list for Danielle."

"I just so happen to have an extra piece of paper right here." Millie plucked the sheet of paper Cat had given her from her pocket. She tore off the part with her current list of suspects, folded it in half and shoved it in her pants pocket. "I don't have a pen."

Andy handed her his pen.

Millie slipped her reading glasses on and began jotting down a list of ship terms:

AFT – Swim aft or stern (back) of the boat.

AGROUND – Run aground. Touching or fast/first to the bottom.

ASTERN - In back of the boat, opposite of ahead.

BOW – Swim to the bow (shallow end) of the pool.

CAPSIZE - To turn over.

FATHOM – How deep is a fathom? (Six feet.)

FORWARD - Toward the bow of the boat.

MIDSHIP - Approximately in the location equally distant from the bow and stern.

PORT – Swim to the port (left) side of the pool.

STARBOARD – Swim to the starboard (right) side of the pool.

STERN – Swim to the stern (deep end) of the pool.

Millie handed the pen to Andy. "We'll need to add some bonus rounds."

"I know." Danielle snapped her fingers. "Whoever can hold their breath longest under water."

"What if they drown?" Andy asked.

"Yeah. Instead of drinking and driving, it will be drinking and drowning," Millie said.

After finishing his lunch, Andy glanced at his watch and pushed back his chair. "I have a meeting with the dancers and singers."

Millie waited until he was out of sight before turning to Danielle. "Remember how you said Isaac was shooting off his mouth in the crew lounge area, saying Brody was going to be gone within 24 hours?"

"Yeah," Danielle said. "I already tried to get him to tell me what he knew but he said we'd find out soon enough. Maybe he was just blowing smoke."

"Can I take another look at the picture of the guy who punched Brody in the face last night?"

"Sure." Danielle pulled her cell phone from her back pocket. "I forgot all about it." She switched her phone on and scrolled through the screen. "It's too far away to see clearly."

Millie slipped her reading glasses on and peered at the picture. It was dark and grainy. "There's no way to tell who it is."

"It was worth a shot." Millie let the subject drop. She didn't want Danielle to start asking questions and find out Millie and Annette planned to go incognito that evening to keep an eye on Brody.

Danielle was impulsive, which was an understatement. The last thing she wanted was for the young woman to tag along.

Little did Millie know Danielle would be the least of her worries.

Chapter 15

Millie, who was carrying her backpack, was the first to arrive at the entrance to deck zero. She hovered off to one side and watched as several crewmembers wandered past, each giving her an odd look.

She briefly wondered if any women worked the night shift. Millie suspected there was not, which meant they would somehow have to come up with a disguise so they wouldn't stand out like sore thumbs.

Cat arrived moments later, still dressed in her work uniform. Millie gave her the once over. She didn't have a maintenance uniform for Cat, which might present a problem.

An uneasy feeling settled over Millie. They were going into this blindly. They didn't know the lay of the land, so-to-speak. She wasn't certain if Brody would be working at the guard gate.

The door leading to the crew maintenance area flew open and Annette leapt out, as if someone was chasing her. She slammed the door shut. "That was a close call."

"You flew in here like someone was chasing you." Cat grinned.

"Almost. I spotted Patterson and Brody in the stairwell one deck up."

Millie's eyes widened. "Did they see you?"

"Nope." Annette shook her head. "At least I don't think they saw me. They were deep in conversation. I tried to listen in but their voices were too low."

"Which means Brody is probably on his way to report to work." Millie grabbed Annette's arm. "We have to hide. Quick!" Her eyes darted around the hall. Directly across from them was a door marked *Go Green*.

"You don't want to go in there," Annette warned, but it was too late. Millie had already opened the door, pushed Cat inside and then dragged Annette in with them before yanking the door shut.

The interior of the confined space was pitch black. Millie's stomach threatened to revolt as the stagnant smell of rotting fish hung heavy in the air. "What is that awful smell?"

"Uneaten passenger food," Annette said.

"It smells like it's been in here for years," Cat gasped.

"No. At most, only a few days." Annette calmly explained Majestic Cruise Lines pureed all uneaten food and when the ship was out to sea, far from land, they released the food into the ocean for the fish and other marine life.

Despite the awful odor, Millie was impressed. "I guess I never thought about what happened to all the wasted food passengers didn't eat or food that spoiled."

"I've read reports that up to 30% of food on board the ship is uneaten," Annette said.

"What a waste," Cat said.

"So you're saying every morsel of food is pureed and then dropped into the ocean as fish food?" Millie whispered.

"Not all. What can't be consumed by marine life is incinerated," Annette said.

A muffled voice echoed in the hall.

"Shh."

The trio stood silently inside the cramped, stinky space. Millie, who was trying to breathe as little as possible since her stomach was still churning, began to feel lightheaded.

The outer hall grew quiet. "I think they're gone." Desperate for fresh air, Millie flung the door open and sprinted into the hall.

Cat followed her out and Annette brought up the rear, quietly closing the door behind them.

"Millie," Cat said. "Your face is as green as the *Go Green* sign."

"I wouldn't doubt it." The lingering odor of rotting food clung to her clothes. "Ugh." She shrugged her backpack off and unzipped the front before reaching inside and pulling out the maintenance uniform. "Hopefully the smell didn't get inside the bag."

Millie lifted the clothes for a quick sniff test and turned to Annette. "Did you bring your uniform?"

"Yep. I put it on under my chef's uniform."

"Great. Why didn't I think of that? Now I'll have to find somewhere to change."

"You could change inside the *Go Green* room," Cat teased.

"Over my dead body." Millie shook her head. "I'd rather strip and change right here in the hall."

"Let's track down this Reef fellow. I'm sure there's a restroom or locker room where you can change," Annette said. "Give Cat your radio so we can contact each other."

Millie unclipped her radio and handed it to her friend.

"What if Andy tries to reach you?" Cat took the radio.

"Don't answer. I typically turn it off after ten," Millie said. "Besides, Andy never tries to radio me this late at night unless it's an emergency." She gave Cat brief instructions on how to operate the radio while Annette did a quick recon of the corridor.

Annette waited until Millie had finished her instructions. "Are you afraid of heights?"

"No." Cat shook her head. "Why?"

Annette pointed at a ladder, hooked to the hall wall and gazed up. At the top of the ladder was a small metal grate, just large enough for a petite person to perch atop. "You'll have a bird's eye view from that vantage point and no one will see you."

"I dunno…"

"You could hide in the *Go Green* room and leave the door open a crack," Millie said.

"The grate it is. Hold this." Cat dropped the radio in Millie's hand and scampered to the top.

Millie handed Cat the radio. "You'll need this too." She fished inside her pocket, pulled out a set of earbuds and tossed them to her friend. "The plug is in the bottom."

"I need a set of those," Annette said.

"We sell them in the store," Cat said as she plugged them in and then hooked the radio's clip to the collar of her shirt. "Ready for action."

Millie circled her thumb and forefinger. "Awesome." She glanced at her watch. "We have five minutes to find Reef and report to work."

With one last glance at Cat, Annette and Millie hurried down the hall in the direction of Sharky's office.

A ray of light beamed from under the door.

Millie paused. "You go first."

Annette tapped lightly before grasping the handle and turning the knob.

At first, it appeared there was no one inside until she noticed a curtained room tucked in the far corner.

"Hello?" Annette said.

The curtain fluttered, shifted to the side and an enormous, hulking man emerged. "Yeah?"

Whatever Millie had envisioned Reef Savage to look like was not what she found, or maybe it was. Her first thought was the man could sit on her and squash her flat.

She watched as he turned sideways, eased out of the small room and lumbered across the floor.

Millie's eyes were drawn to his face and one feature in particular - a patch that covered his eye.

She leaned forward for a closer look and realized it wasn't an actual eye patch, but a tattoo of a patch.

"What're you starin' at?"

"I. Your eye," she said bluntly. "I've never seen anyone with a tattoo patch on their eye."

"You like it?" The man smiled and rubbed his eye. "Cost me a pretty penny, that one." He changed the subject. "Sharky warned me a couple gals would be comin' round this evening to work the night shift. Which one of you is Millie?"

Millie raised her hand. "You must be Reef."

"Yes ma'am." Reef nodded. "Where's my grub?"

"Grub?"

"Food. Sharky said you'd be bringing me some gourmet grub in exchange for babysittin' you two for the night."

"We paid Sharky with food," Annette explained. "We had no idea we'd have to bring more food."

"No food, no workee."

It was too late to run upstairs and prepare a meal for Reef without losing precious time. "Tell you what, you let us work tonight and right before the shift ends, I'll bring you back the biggest plate of fish and chips you've ever seen," Annette bargained.

Reef rubbed his chin thoughtfully.

"What have you got to lose?" Millie asked.

"True. You're right about that. Okay," Reef relented. "I guess I'll have to trust you to keep your end of the bargain."

He eyed Millie's jeans and cotton blouse. "You look like you're goin' to a Sunday picnic, not workin' the graveyard shift in the pit."

"My clothes are in my backpack," Millie said. "I haven't changed yet."

"You can change in there." Reef pointed to the small room he'd just come out of.

Millie frowned as she eyed the room nervously.

"It's either change in there or I can show you where the men's toilet is located."

"I'll be right back." Millie darted into the corner room and pulled the curtain shut. She checked for gaps before slipping out of her street clothes and throwing the uniform on. Since Sharky hadn't offered her work shoes, she'd worn her sneakers in case she had to make a run for it.

She shoved her clothes into the backpack and zipped it shut before rejoining Reef and Annette.

Reef sank into the office chair and it groaned loudly in protest.

Millie cringed as she waited for it to collapse under Reef's expansive girth. "We'll have to do somethin' about your girlie hair."

He opened one of the desk drawers, fumbled around inside and pulled out two black stocking caps and hard hats. "This'll have to do."

"Thanks." Millie tucked her hair under the cap before easing the hard hat on top and securing the chinstrap.

Reef reached for a clipboard, hanging on the wall. "Sharky mentioned something about working near the nightshift security guards."

"Yes. Specifically near the security supervisor," Annette said.

"That would be..." Reef's voice trailed off as he studied the clipboard. "Brody Rourke." He lifted a brow. "You sure you wanna work over there? I heard there's trouble brewing tonight. Some kind of rumble between maintenance and security. Things might get out of hand."

"We're sure," Millie said firmly.

"He's working in zones four, five and six. We're using zone seven for storage. There's a lot of stuff over there so I would avoid the area unless you have a flashlight." Reef stood. "I'm still disappointed about no food."

Annette cut him off. "I can assure you, we'll make good on our end of the deal."

"I guess I have no choice. Follow me." Reef reluctantly motioned them out of the room and into the corridor.

Millie caught a glimpse of Cat, perched on the metal grate and winked as they passed by. They walked the entire length of the ship until they reached the crew exit where a large number "6" was spray painted on the dock.

"This is it," Reef announced as he abruptly stopped. "Are you sticking around for the whole shift?"

Annette and Millie glanced at each other. "We're not sure," Millie said.

"Well, don't forget about our deal. You'll need to return the uniforms when you're done. Make sure they're clean." Reef abruptly walked away, the bottom of his work boots creating a dull *thud* on the corridor floor.

"He was about as charming as a cranky crab," Annette said.

"Right?" Millie stepped off the ship and onto the dock. The evening air was damp and cool. She shivered and sucked in a breath of fresh air as she remembered the putrid smell of the *Go Green* room. "Let's start in zone four and then work our way back here to zone six."

Zone four was near the front of the ship. One of the ship's massive anchors moved up and down as a group of workers stood watching.

A few feet away another group of workers were cleaning and polishing a row of luggage carts. "They've got these guys working round the clock," Annette said.

The women slowly circled zones four and five several times, as they searched for Brody.

When they drew close to the entrance checkpoint, Millie motioned Annette off to the side. "I don't see Brody."

"Me either. Maybe he's still inside."

Millie shifted her gaze. A few yards away, a crowd had gathered. She couldn't see what they were staring at but her heart sank when she realized they were standing in front of what would be the ship's rock-climbing wall. "Something's going on over there."

When the women reached the edge of the crowd, Millie bounced on her heels as she tried to catch a glimpse of what they were looking at. She finally gave up and squeezed past several of the onlookers.

When she reached the front, Millie gazed in horror at the body of a lifeless man, dangling from the end of a long rope.

Chapter 16

Brody was to the left of her. He yelled at the workers to cut the man down but Millie's gut told her it was too late.

Annette, who had followed Millie to the front, pulled her radio from her belt. "Medic needed at zone seven." Before the words were out of her mouth, the medical crew arrived on scene.

"Move aside." Brody waved his hands. "Give them room."

"There's Patterson. Let's get out of here." Annette slipped into the crowd.

Millie began to back up, praying that Patterson hadn't seen them. She took several steps back and accidentally stepped on someone's foot.

"Sorry." Millie glanced over her shoulder. "Danielle?"

"Millie?" Danielle's eyes narrowed. "I almost didn't recognize you. What in the world?" Her voice trailed off. "I should've guessed. You're out here spying on Brody."

"I'm trying to keep him safe," Millie said.

Danielle tugged on Millie's arm and they stepped away from the crowd.

Annette wandered over to join them.

"You were in on it too?" Danielle asked. "Did you see what happened?"

"I was going to ask you the same thing," Millie said. "We were over near the gate when we noticed a crowd gathering in zone seven."

"I was inside working on the new pool games when I heard something on the radio. I looked for you earlier and when I couldn't find you, I figured somehow you were involved," Danielle said. "Did you recognize the person?"

"Nope." Millie shook her head. "When Patterson arrived, we got outta there."

Woop. Woop.

Flashing lights and the sound of sirens filled the air. An ambulance arrived on scene and came to a screeching halt near the gate.

The ambulance doors flew open and two EMTs raced to the rock-climbing wall. A short time later, one of them made his way to the back of the ambulance. When he returned, he was carrying a stretcher.

Millie made her way to the fence where she had a clear view of the ambulance. A short time later, she watched as the crowd parted for the EMTs. They carried the covered stretcher through the gate to the back of the ambulance.

After sliding the stretcher in the back, they returned to the front of the ambulance and climbed inside. They shut their lights off before backing up and slowly driving off.

"DOA," Danielle said.

"Hey." She stopped two of the crewmembers who were walking away. "Any idea who bit the big one?"

"Isaac Ris- something."

"No way," Danielle turned to Millie and Annette. "Where's Brody?"

"My guess is talking to the port authorities," Annette said. "He was already here when we got here."

"I hope you have an alibi for him," Danielle said. "Because the guy dangling from the wall was the big mouth in the crew bar the other night who was telling everyone Brody was going to be off the ship in 24 hours or less."

"And quite possibly the one who punched Brody last night." Millie watched as the crowd began to disperse. "We better get out of here," she muttered under her breath.

The women casually strolled toward the crew entrance when Reef's voice rang out. "...and I sent these two ladies out here. They were disguised in night shift uniforms and looking for your head of night security."

Millie stopped in her tracks. "Uh-oh."

"What two women?" Patterson asked in a hard voice.

It was too late. They were in Patterson's unobstructed line of vision.

Millie could feel the heat of Patterson's stare creep up her neck. She slowly turned to face the man she'd hoped to avoid.

"Millie Sanders."   She could tell by the tone of Patterson's voice he wasn't pleased.

"Busted," Annette whispered under her breath. "I'll catch up with you later."

"And Annette Delacroix," Patterson added.

Danielle shrank back but Patterson's sharp eye didn't miss a thing. "Where's your disguise Danielle?"

"I don't have a disguise and I'm as shocked as you are," Danielle said.

"Traitor," Millie hissed as the trio made their way over. Brody, who was standing nearby, turned.

"Millie? Is that you?" Brody squinted his eyes and studied Millie from head to toe. "What are you doing out here?"

"My guess is that they were trying to keep an eye on you," Patterson said. "Not only did it backfire, but now I'll have to bring all of you in for questioning."

"Not me," Danielle protested. "I had nothing to do with this. Ask your informant there. He can tell you I wasn't involved."

"Never seen her before in my life," Reef agreed. "She's a looker. I would've remembered her."

Danielle shot him a dirty look before facing Patterson. "So I'm free to go?"

"No." Patterson shook his head. "I think you're somehow involved in Millie's scheme."

"Scheme," Millie sputtered. "It wasn't a scheme."

"I would describe this one as more of a passive observational project," Annette said.

"Call it whatever you want," Patterson said. "I want all three of you in my office in exactly one hour."

"Aye, aye." Annette gave Patterson a mock salute. "We'll be there."

"Great," Danielle muttered as they walked toward the crew gangway. "Now look what you've gotten me into."

Millie ignored the comment as she led the way inside and down the long hall to the back of the ship. "We might as well ditch the uniforms."

"Psst."

Danielle grabbed Millie's arm. "Did you hear that?"

"Cat," Annette and Millie said in unison.

"I almost forgot about her," Millie said as she darted to the side of the corridor and looked up.

"What happened? You're back already?"

"Cat?" Danielle watched in disbelief as Cat slowly crawled from her crouched position and backed down the ladder.

"What are you doing here?" Cat swiped at the seat of her pants.

"What am I doing here? Wait a minute." Danielle wagged her finger at Millie. "You. The three of you cooked up this undercover scheme but didn't bother to include me, yet I'm the one getting called out on the carpet by Patterson for this dude's death?"

Cat's hand flew to her mouth. "Brody is dead?"

"No. Not Brody. It was another guy," Annette said. "It's a long story."

"But you've only been gone less than an hour," Cat said.

"I'm surprised myself," Millie said. "Let's go change." The women finished their short walk to Sharky/Reef's office. The door was unlocked so the women let themselves in.

"Did you see someone die?" Cat asked. "I heard men in the corridor talking about medical being called to the storage area in zone seven. I kept praying it wasn't Brody or one of you."

"It was a guy named Isaac." Danielle slumped into one of the chairs.

Millie removed the hard hat and cap. "What if Reef set us up?" She grabbed the backpack she'd left on one of the office chairs and slipped into the small corner room before pulling the curtain shut.

Annette removed the crew shirt, pulled her chef's jacket on and began buttoning the front. "That's a strong possibility if you think about it. Maybe he was gunning for Brody's job."

"He set Brody up to take the fall for Isaac's death." Millie slipped her shoes on and pulled the curtain to the side. "Think about it. Brody's attack happened during the night shift."

"Maybe it had nothing at all to do with the red light district," Cat chimed in. "All along, Reef plotted to get rid of Brody."

Danielle twirled a strand of hair around her fingers. "He thought he could scare him into quitting by having one of his guys jump Brody and when that didn't work, Reef decided to set him up."

She went on. "Maybe Reef found out Isaac was shooting off his mouth the other night, bragging Brody would be gone in 24 hours or less. He decided to kill two birds with one stone...silence Isaac and make it look like Brody did it."

Millie draped the maintenance uniform on an empty chair. "I wouldn't rule out Sharky either."

The door flew open and Reef traipsed into the office. "I thought you two would be long gone."

"We had to drop off the uniforms," Millie said. "Thanks for throwing us under the bus. We didn't have anything to do with the guy's death."

"I don't know that," Reef said. "For all I know, you planned to set Brody up. Two things are certain...you were at the scene of the crime and wearing disguises."

"Like we had time to kill the man, tie a rope around his neck and toss him over the side of the rock-climbing wall," Annette argued.

"Take it up with Dave Patterson." Reef turned to Cat. "Who are you?"

"A friend," Cat's eyes were transfixed on Reef's tattooed eye patch. "Let's get out of here." The tattoo was creeping her out.

"So what time are you coming by with my food? My shift ends at ten tomorrow morning."

"We aren't bringing you a darn thing," Millie said.

"But." Reef's mouth fell open. "A deal is a deal. I skipped eating in the crew mess because I thought you were bringing me fish and chips." He stared at Annette accusingly. "You lied."

"And you blew our cover," Annette said. "You failed to live up to your end of the bargain."

Reef let loose a string of cuss words while Cat, Annette and Danielle hurried out of the office.

Millie was the last to leave. "I hope you don't kiss your mother with that mouth."

Reef's face twisted into a mask of rage and he took a menacing step in Millie's direction. She bolted from the room and slammed the door in his face. "Let's go. I think he's ticked off."

The women jogged down the hall toward the exit. Thankfully, Reef didn't follow behind.

When they reached the safety of deck one, they stopped on the landing. "I want to go back outside," Millie said. "I'd like to take a closer look at zone seven."

"I'll go with you," Danielle said.

"We have half an hour before we have to report to Patterson's office," Annette said.

"Do I have to go?" Cat asked.

"Did you see anything while you were hanging out in the hall?" Millie turned to her friend.

"You mean hanging from the rafters?" Cat joked. "No. The only thing I heard was medic being called. I saw a few workers walking up and down the hall but nothing appeared out of the ordinary. Of course, I'm not familiar with the night shift's routine. So what exactly happened?"

Millie briefly explained how Reef had walked them to the exit and pointed out Brody's work zones, how they'd started searching for Brody near the front before slowly making their way back. It was near zone seven where they noticed a crowd had gathered and when they got close, discovered a person dangling from the wall.

Annette picked up. "When Patterson showed up, which was right after we did, we tried to hang back to avoid detection. That's when our new pal, Reef, spotted us and told Patterson we were in the vicinity, disguised as maintenance workers."

"Unfortunately, Brody was there before us," Millie said.

"Which makes him the perfect suspect," Cat said.

"What if Isaac planned to murder Brody but the plan backfired and he ended up accidentally killing himself?" Danielle said.

It was possible. At this point, anything was possible.

"We have Hugh, not to mention Nevlin, Brody's cabin mate, and Reef," Millie ticked off the list of suspects.

"And Sharky," Annette said. "Sharky mentioned he'd heard rumors of an attack."

"True," Millie agreed. "It seems like we're going in circles and it could be almost anyone." She glanced at her watch. "We're running out of time if we want to scope out the scene of the crime."

"I'll tag along," Cat said.

"I'll go," Danielle said.

"Me too," Annette chimed in. "Four heads are better than one."

"I suppose you want your radio back." Cat unclipped Millie's radio and handed it to her. She turned to Danielle. "I'm sorry you felt left out. I'm sure Millie and Annette just didn't think to include you this time."

"Fat chance," Danielle said.

The women headed up the steps to the other employee gangway. Millie wanted to avoid another run in with Reef.

"That dude's tattoo is creepy," Danielle said.

"You mean Reef's eye patch tattoo? It is a little unsettling if you stare at it long enough," Millie agreed. "Isn't that the kind of tattoo ex-cons get?"

"Nah." Annette waved a hand. "Ex-pirate maybe. Ex-con – doubtful. Majestic Cruise Lines would never hire an ex-con."

"Prison tattoos run more along the line of dots," Danielle said.

"Mi vida loca," Annette said. "My crazy life."

"Or cobwebs, which mean a lengthy prison sentence."

"So a pirate's patch is not popular with convicts?" Millie asked.

Annette shrugged. "Like I said, Majestic would never hire someone with a rap sheet."

When they reached the dock, they quickly canvassed the entire area but came up empty-handed.

"We better head back downstairs to meet Patterson," Millie said.

"Yeah. He won't be happy if we're late," Annette said.

When they reached Patterson's office, the door was wide open. "I was just getting ready to call you on the radio."

Chapter 17

Millie took the seat closest to the door.

Danielle plopped down in the middle seat. "For the record, I protest having to be here. I had nothing to do with this evening's events. Not one iota." She stressed *iota*.

"Duly noted." Patterson turned to Cat. "Look what the cat dragged in. Don't tell me you're involved in this incident as well."

"You could say I was just a silent observer."

Danielle snorted.

Millie gave her a hard look before turning to Patterson. "We have nothing to hide."

"Tell me what happened from the moment you decided to take it upon yourselves to become involved in Brody's situation, which has now turned into a murder investigation."

"So the young man's death wasn't an accident?" Annette asked innocently.

Patterson rubbed his chin. "Not unless he decided to climb to the top of the rock-climbing wall and tie one end of a rope around his neck before jumping off in a dramatic suicide scene. Who wants to start?"

"I'll go first," Danielle said. "I was working on new passenger activities up on the lido deck when I heard someone from medical being called to dock zone seven so I dropped everything and ran down to see what had happened. End of story."

"Medic has been called out several times since we've been in dry dock. Are you an ambulance chaser now?"

Danielle frowned. "No. This was the first time I decided to check it out."

"Were you concerned somehow Millie was involved?" Patterson pressed.

"I object," Millie interjected.

Patterson lifted a brow. "On what grounds?"

"You're trying to lead the witness," Millie said.

"Overruled."

Danielle cast Millie an uneasy glance. Touched by her young friend's loyalty, Millie reached over and squeezed her hand. "It's okay Danielle. You can tell Patterson why you were there."

She turned to face her interrogator. "Danielle is telling the truth. She had nothing to do with our surveillance operation. She had been looking for me and when she couldn't find me and heard the radio call, she was worried something had happened and somehow I was involved."

"With good reason," Patterson said. "You've never lied before. Bent the truth maybe, but outright lying is not part of your DNA." He turned to Danielle. "You're free to go."

"I might as well stay now. I mean, I'm already here and I'd like to hear what happened."

"Suit yourself."

Millie explained how they had learned the victim had been boasting Brody would be off the ship within 24 hours.

"Boasting about Brody?" That got Patterson's attention and he sat upright in his seat. "Isaac Risang?"

"Correct." Millie nodded. "So we decided to keep an eye on Brody to make sure nothing happened. I got the bright idea to borrow night shift maintenance uniforms and kind of, you know, stay out of the way, more of silent observers."

"Keep our noses clean for once," Annette added.

Patterson held up a fist. "I can count on one hand the number of times that has happened...zero."

He leaned back in his chair. "Reef Savage went along with your plan?"

"It took a little negotiating," Millie said. "But the answer is yes. He loaned us the uniforms." She quickly decided to leave Sharky out of it. Technically, he had been the middleman.

"In exchange for?" Patterson prompted.

"Food," Annette said. "Fish and chips to be exact." She hurried on. "Reef walked us to the exit, pointed out the areas the night shift and security crew were working and then went back inside."

Millie picked up. "Reef told us no one was working in zone seven, the storage zone where the rock-climbing wall was located so we walked to the front of the ship and worked our way back. We made it as far as zone six when we noticed a crowd had gathered near the storage zone and when we got close, we saw the victim."

She went on. "Reef told us to avoid zone seven, which leads me to believe he needs to be questioned."

"When you first walked outside, did you notice anything unusual, any crew acting strangely?" Patterson asked.

"No. In fact, I remember looking at the storage zone and the area appeared empty," Annette said.

"How long was it between the time Reef showed you the work zones and when you noticed the crowd?"

"I checked my watch before we headed to the first zone. It was right around eleven fifteen." Annette drummed her fingers on the desk. "I would say a good forty-five minutes between the time Reef left us and the time we noticed the crowd."

"Where was Brody?"

Annette and Millie exchanged a quick glance. "When we first exited the ship, we couldn't find him, but on the way back, we noticed he was standing in zone seven, radio in hand. I guess he had already called medical and you."

"Was he near the front of the crowd or the back of the crowd?" Patterson asked.

Millie sucked in a breath and closed her eyes, fully aware her next words would not help Brody's case. "He was near the front and not far from the victim."

"So he had to be one of the first on scene. Is there anything else you'd like to tell me?"

"I don't think Brody did it," Millie said. "I'm gonna put my money on Reef Savage. It was the perfect set up."

"He would certainly have opportunity, keeping his night crew away from zone seven and the storage area," Patterson said. "What is his motive?"

"I haven't figured that out yet. All I know is Brody's first attack was in the maintenance area. Isaac, the victim, worked in maintenance and now this. It all happened during the night shift." Millie shifted in her chair. "Think about it. Brody would be the perfect scapegoat. Maybe this had to do with Isaac all along."

"Everyone involved will be questioned." Patterson stood...his signal the meeting had ended. "You two still aren't off the hook. I'm considering writing you both up for impersonating a crewmember."

"Flawed logic," Annette said. "We are crew."

He pointed his finger at Annette. "Don't tempt me."

After the women exited the office, Danielle, the last to leave, wiped her hand across her brow. "That was a close one."

"We still aren't out of the woods," Annette said. "It's time to put our heads together. We're missing something, some piece of the puzzle. I have just the thing to get our wheels spinning."

"What's that?"

"Cooking," Annette said. "Let's head to the galley. I've been tinkering with my chocolate melting cake and need some taste testers."

Chapter 18

It was well past midnight by the time the women reached the galley.

Annette pulled a tray of ramekin dishes from the cupboard and slid the tray onto the counter. "Grab a couple bags of dark chocolate chips out of my office."

Millie hurried to the large walk-in pantry aka Annette's office.

"And some white sugar and flour."

"I'll help." Danielle followed Millie into the pantry.

Annette sent Cat to the refrigerator in search of a tub of butter while she headed to the spice pantry for the vanilla extract.

"What if."

Annette held up a hand. "Wait until I mix the ingredients together. Otherwise I'll be making chocolate melting pudding instead of cake."

The group silently watched as Annette stuck a saucepan on the stove and turned the burner on before measuring the chocolate chips and butter.

While the chips melted, she preheated the oven and dumped the remaining ingredients into a large mixing bowl. She grabbed her whisk. "Coast is clear. Yack away."

Millie kept an eye on the chocolate chips and butter. Once the chips melted, she shut the burner off and carried the pan to the counter.

"Thanks," Annette said. "When it cools a little, I'll mix everything together and pour it into the dishes."

"We can work on whittling down our list of suspects," Danielle said. "Who's left now that Isaac is gone?"

"We have Nevlin, Brody's cabin mate, Hugh, the guy in the bar with Isaac, Reef and Brody." Millie rattled off the list. "I hate to say it but Brody is either one of the unluckiest guys in the whole world or someone is doing an excellent job of making his life unbearable."

"I would go with the latter," Annette said. "Don't forget to add Sharky."

"Reef gets my vote." Danielle shivered. "I still can't get the visual of that creepy tattoo patch out of my head."

"It's possible the man who hanged himself committed suicide," Cat said. "What if he was in love with Brody and Brody shunned his advances so he killed himself?"

"That's a possibility," Millie said. "Brody swears he's not interested in men. Maybe Brody sent off the wrong signals. Ticked off, Isaac attacked him in an attempt to get him to fight back, figuring Patterson would fire him. "

"If this is the end of the incidents, then I guess we can safely say Isaac was behind the attacks and did himself in," Danielle said. "He seemed confident Brody would be the one gone."

"We can't forget Brody's claim of a person lying on the corridor floor who mysteriously vanished but left behind a pool of blood," Millie said.

Annette poured the chocolate into the mixing bowl and began stirring. "What if Brody is covering for someone? Follow me here. What if Brody went to the red light district to help a friend who was in a tight situation?"

"That makes a ton more sense," Millie said. "He swears up and down he's not interested in men, yet eyewitnesses saw him at the gay bar. I can see him coming to a friend's rescue."

"Or even a cabin mate," Cat said. "What do you know about his cabin mate?"

"Not much," Millie said. "His name is Nevlin and he works night security."

"Cat, how long has the employee swipe card tracking system been working?" Millie asked.

"A few days."

"Was it working when we were in San Juan?"

"Nope." Cat shook her head. "I'm afraid not."

The women discussed the suspects at length but even after the decadent chocolate dessert had finished baking, they still weren't any closer to figuring out who had attacked Brody and killed Isaac.

Millie covered a yawn as Annette passed out the fresh-from-the-oven treats. "I'll grab some ice cream." She returned with a large tub of French vanilla ice cream and scooped a spoonful on the top of each of the desserts.

Fragrant steam rose from the center as Millie reached for a spoon and dipped it into the decadent treat. "Oh my gosh. This is delicious," she said. "I can feel the pounds packing on."

"Me too," Cat murmured between bites. "I'm not sure what the dessert tasted like before, but you've got a winner on your hands, Annette."

"I tried a different type of chocolate. This one has a higher percentage of cacao," Annette said. "Sometimes even the smallest change can make a big difference."

"You nailed it," Danielle said.

The women finished their chocolate dessert, all proclaiming it one of the best ever.

"You're right, if I do say so myself." Annette beamed. "Plus it's super easy and has only a few ingredients."

They made quick work of cleaning up their mess and then made their way into the hall.

Millie glanced at her watch, relieved they hadn't stuck around for an entire night shift. She wasn't sure she would have been able to stay awake, although a lot of caffeine and perhaps an extra dose of chocolate cake might have helped.

When the women reached their cabin, Millie perched on the edge of her bunk while she waited for Danielle to get ready for bed.

Her thoughts drifted to Nevlin, Brody's cabin mate. He seemed to know enough to warn Brody he was in danger.

After Danielle emerged, they traded places. Tomorrow would be a busy day. Millie needed to work on new trivia contests, meet with Andy to see if he'd come up with more tasks for them to complete while they were in dry dock and then hopefully talk to Brody again - if he wasn't in jail, charged with Isaac's murder.

She woke early the next morning with a large knot in the pit of her stomach. It was the feeling she got whenever she knew something bad was about to happen, like waiting for the other shoe to drop, and not in a good way.

Danielle was up unusually early and instead of being grouchy, she was chipper. She even offered to grab some coffee while Millie got ready, which Millie readily accepted.

Not only did Danielle bring back coffee, she brought back a tray, laden with enticing breakfast treats. Millie realized she'd missed dinner the previous night, and despite the feeling of foreboding, she devoured her food.

While they ate, the women discussed the new pool activities and all of the items they would need to purchase before the ship set sail.

After they finished, they stopped by the crew mess to drop their dirty dishes in the bin before climbing the stairs to the lido deck to scope out locations.

The morning flew by and as the hours passed, Millie's uneasiness began to subside. She was still determined to track down Brody to confront him with her suspicions he was covering for someone but figured he would be sleeping. She still hadn't formulated a plan on how to broach the subject.

Danielle and Millie had just finished their meticulous material list they planned to run by Andy for approval when Millie's radio began squawking. "Millie, do you copy?"

Millie frowned at the sound of Dave Patterson's voice. "Now what?" she asked Danielle before lifting the radio and pressing the button. "This is Millie. Go ahead."

"Please meet me in my office."

"Now?"

"Yes. Now."

"I'm on my way." Millie hung her head as she clipped her radio to her belt. The proverbial other shoe had dropped.

Chapter 19

The first thing Millie noticed when she stepped inside Patterson's office was Sharky Kiveski seated across from Patterson. His face was beet red and he was breathing hard.

The second thing she noticed was she wasn't the only one who had been summoned to Patterson's office. Annette was there looking none too pleased.

"Thank you for joining us," Patterson motioned toward the door. "Please. Close the door behind you and have a seat."

Annette sat on one side. Sharky sat on the other. The seat in the middle was empty so Millie dragged it close to Annette. Patterson waited until Millie was seated before speaking.

"I just left Mr. Kiveski's office."

"It's a nice office," Annette said.

Patterson gave her a dark look and cleared his throat. "It *was* a nice office. Someone vandalized it while Sharky was making his rounds this morning."

He leaned in. "Do either of you have any idea who might've done that?"

"No. Millie shook her head. "Not at all."

"Sharky seems to think you do."

"That's crazy," Millie sputtered. "Why would we tear your place apart?"

"Because Reef fingered you two as having something to do with Isaac's death last night," Sparky said. "Not only that, ever since you two broads showed up…"

"Mr. Kiveski," Patterson warned.

Sharky rolled his eyes. "Okay, ever since you two *ladies* showed up in my office, it's been nothing but trouble. It's either you or Brody Rourke."

"Brody is asleep in his cabin," Patterson said as he turned his attention to Millie. "Do you have an alibi for your whereabouts this morning?"

"Of course." Millie nodded. "I've been with Danielle, going over the plans for the new lido deck activities."

"What about you?" he asked Annette.

"I've been in the galley working on lunch. Several of the kitchen crew can vouch for me, including Amit. I haven't left the kitchen all morning."

"That clears one of you. You're free to go."

"Not without Millie," Annette said. "You know there's no way she trashed Sharky's office. I mean, not without a good reason."

"Thanks for trying to help." Millie patted her friend's hand.

Patterson grabbed his radio and turned up the volume. "Danielle. Do you copy?"

"Go ahead."

"Where have you been all morning?"

"I've been up on lido with Millie. We've been going over the plans for the new outdoor activities."

Millie shot Sharky a triumphant look.

"She could be lying," Sharky muttered. "I'm willing to let this whole thing slide if she comes to my office and cleans up the mess."

"I." Millie was about to say "refuse" but changed her mind. Maybe it was a blessing in disguise. Perhaps there was some hidden clue inside Sharky's office, something that would lead her to who was behind Brody's attacks and Isaac's death. "I'll do it."

"Are you sure?" Patterson asked. "You both have alibis." He turned to Sharky. "It could be a disgruntled employee. Have you written anyone up lately?"

"I write people up on a daily basis, but they've never trashed my office before. I still say it's got something to do with these two," Sharky insisted.

"I'll help," Annette offered. "It's time for my break anyway."

Sharky stood. "You coming?"

"I'll need to change first," Millie said as she pointed at her white slacks.

"Me too." Annette glanced at her spotless chef's uniform.

"I'll be waiting," was Sharky's parting shot before exiting Patterson's office.

Annette flipped him the bird.

"Annette," Millie said.

"He's a jerk."

"True, but you have to admit, he's got a point," Millie said.

"Try not to aggravate Sharky while you clean up his office," Patterson warned.

"Of course not. You know we wouldn't do that," Annette said sarcastically. "He's our new best bud. Him and his pal, Reef, who by the way, ought to be at the top of your list of suspects."

"He's there," Patterson said. "We're already working with the port police to determine the cause of Mr. Risang's unfortunate demise."

"Do you think he committed suicide?" Millie had to ask.

"It's possible. We're not ruling anything out." Patterson sighed heavily. "The fact Isaac was telling everyone Brody was about to get canned casts suspicion on him. I'm not sure if I'll be able to get him off the hook this time."

Millie briefly explained her theory, how she thought Brody might be covering for a friend by taking the heat and taking the beatings.

"Reef Savage seemed all too anxious to throw Annette and me under the bus last night. He had opportunity to arrange for Brody's attack and who's to say he didn't trash his own office just to throw the investigators off?"

"I agree," Patterson said. "We'll be looking closely at Reef, not to mention Brody and Brody's cabin mate. There's also Hugh someone but I'm not sure how he fits into the picture."

"We better get going before Sharky throws a hissy fit," Annette said.

The women parted ways to change into old work clothes and then met up at the stairwell.

"Let me guess. You agreed to clean Sharky's office because you want to snoop."

"Bingo," Millie said. "This will give us the perfect opportunity to look around. Someone was looking for something inside Sharky/Reef's office."

"I hoped maybe this Isaac guy's death was tied to Brody's attacks and last night was the end of it," Annette said.

"Me too. I guess it was wishful thinking on our part."

Sharky was standing in the center of his office when the women arrived. "I was just about to call you on the radio. Look at this place."

Strewn across Sharky's desk and floor were sheets of paper. His desk drawers were wide open. One of the filing cabinet doors was bent.

Sharky followed Millie's gaze. "Someone tried to pry open the cabinet."

The water cooler in the corner was tipped at an odd angle and a puddle of water had soaked a pile of papers scattered on the floor. Even the mini fridge behind the desk had been ransacked, its contents carelessly piled off to one side.

"I'm leaving for a couple hours and when I get back, this place better be spic and span or else."

"Or else what?" Millie couldn't help herself.

"I'm filing a complaint and taking it all the way to the top, to Captain Armati!"

Annette snickered and Millie elbowed her. "We'll have it clean."

Sharky hopped on his scooter, flipped the switch and with a big bang backfire, roared out of the office and out of sight.

"Good riddance," Annette said as she closed the door behind him. "Now. Where do we start?"

"Let's start with the water cooler." They tipped the water cooler upright and dried the floor and papers with a stack of shop towels they found stacked in the corner of the small changing room.

The women worked in silence as they snooped and cleaned, moving as quickly and thoroughly as possible as they searched for clues.

They organized the papers first, stacking them in tidy piles on the desk before salvaging as much of the refrigerated items as possible. "I'm gonna go out on a limb and say that Sharky will expect us to replenish the stuff we had to toss out."

"Yeah, a half-eaten box of ho ho's, a block of moldy Colby cheese and this." Millie held up what looked like a petri dish full of fungus. "Disgusting." She dropped the dish in the trash bag and turned her attention to the filing cabinet.

"Someone wanted to get inside this cabinet pretty bad," Millie said as she ran her finger along the edge of the twisted metal.

Annette shoved her hands on her hips and gazed at the tidy office. "It looks like our job here is done."

"I think it's cleaner now than before someone trashed it," Millie said.

Annette started to answer when the sound of tires squealing caught her attention. "He's baaack."

Sharky appeared in the doorway, peering inside. "This looks a little better."

"A little better?" Millie asked. "No. It looks a lot better." She pointed to the stacks of papers on the desk. "We didn't know where to put these so we just stacked them up."

Sharky ignored Millie and shuffled to the back of the room where he opened the refrigerator door. "You're gonna replace my stuff, right?"

"Not our responsibility," Annette said.

Sharky slammed the door shut. "You might as well have admitted responsibility. Who in their right mind would clean up this mess unless they made it in the first place?"

"Unless they wanted to snoop," Millie muttered under her breath.

"Yeah, well you wasted your time." He pointed at the damaged file cabinet drawer. "All the good stuff, the employee dirt, is locked in there."

Annette ignored the comment and marched to the door. "Our job here is done."

"No hard feelings? Right?" Sharky hurried after them.

"You jerk," Annette said.

252

Sharky shrugged. "Eh. I've been called worse. So the next time you need a favor, you'll keep ole Sharkster in mind? That was a tasty dinner the other night." He patted his protruding stomach.

Annette opened her mouth but Millie reached out to stop her. "Of course. You never know when we'll need another favor."

"Over my dead body," Annette growled.

"That's what I thought." Sharky held the door. "Watch out for my scooter."

The women slipped past the flaming scooter and headed to the exit.

"I do believe Sharky may have given me my 'ah ha' moment. It was sitting back there, right on the edge of my mind. When he walked in and started looking around, it dawned on me."

"You mean as far as cracking the case?"

"There's a strong possibility that Brody stumbled upon something he shouldn't have and there really was a body." Millie nodded. "I know just the person who might be able to help crack this case."

"Who is that?"

"Cat."

Chapter 20

Annette and Millie searched high and low for Cat. The first place they tried was the gift shop, after that, her cabin, and then every other area. "Where could she be?" Millie was stumped.

"You don't think she got off the ship," Annette said.

"I have an idea." Cat was making progress in venturing off the ship in ports but so far, Millie was sure she hadn't explored Miami unless she was with Joe, Doctor Gundervan. "Let's check medical."

"Great idea. We can see if Doctor Gundervan has any information on Isaac's death while we're there." The women descended the stairs until they reached deck two. The ship's medical center was on the same deck as security as well as the ship's morgue.

The door was unlocked so they stepped inside the small waiting room. It was empty. The tinkling of a woman's laughter echoed from the examination room.

"Anybody home?" Millie hollered toward the back.

The laughter stopped and Cat emerged, her face flushed. "Hi Millie. Annette." She smoothed her hair and stepped into the waiting room.

Doctor Gundervan followed her out, looking like a school kid who had just been busted. "Hello Millie." He nodded to Annette. "Annette."

"Where's Rachel?" Rachel was the ship's nurse and gossip extraordinaire.

"She's upstairs on break," Doctor Gundervan said.

"Ah." Annette lifted a brow. "Cat thought the good doctor might be lonely so she thought she'd keep you company without nurse busybody taking notes."

"I was just getting ready to leave." Cat turned to her beau. "We're meeting tomorrow at ten just outside the gangway?"

"Yes. Don't forget your sunscreen and swimsuit in case we decide to hop off at the beach." Doctor Gundervan gave Cat a quick peck on the lips. "Now which one of you ladies needs my assistance?"

"Neither. We were actually looking for Cat."

"Oh." Doctor Gundervan cast Cat a quick glance. "You need her for another spy mission?"

"Cat," Millie admonished.

"What? He's not going to tell anyone."

"While we're here, is there any news on the poor deceased man?" Annette asked.

Gundervan shook his head. "You know I can't discuss the case. All I can say is I'm almost positive there's still an open investigation into Mr. Risang's death."

Cat blew her beau a kiss before following Annette and Millie into the hall.

Annette pulled the door shut. "Where's lover boy taking you tomorrow?"

"Somewhere called Lincoln Road. It's a shopping area near Miami Beach. We're going to have lunch and do a little sightseeing."

"It sounds like fun." Millie changed the subject. "I was wondering if I could take a look at your computer again."

Cat frowned. "You can't log onto the employee computers? I heard the connection is lightning fast now that we're docked in port."

"No. I need *your* computer."

"Ah." Cat lifted a brow. "I see. You want to take a look at the log."

"Yeah. Do you still have access?"

"As far as I know."

The trio hurried up the steps and when they reached Ocean Treasures, Cat unlocked the door and motioned them inside. "I'm sure any day now Donovan is going to figure out the site isn't secure and he'll block it."

"I still don't know what we're doing," Annette grumbled.

"You'll see in a minute," Millie promised.

Cat made her way to the back of the newly renovated gift shop.

"You did a great job re-designing this place," Millie complimented.

"Thanks." Cat turned her computer on, swiped her access card and then reached for her glasses. "You're in luck. I still have access." Cat tapped the keyboard. "Who or what are we looking for?"

"First, I want to check Brody's movements since the first night he was attacked."

Millie peeked over Cat's shoulder as she studied the screen. "He's pretty consistent, starting his shift at eleven p.m. and then clocking out at ten a.m."

"Whew." Annette blew air through thinned lips. "Now that's an all-nighter."

"Yeah. Eleven hours is a long shift," Cat agreed.

"Were you ever able to hear anything on the listening device you hid in Brody's cabin?" Millie asked.

Annette tapped her pocket. "I've been listening off and on, whenever I have a break but so far, there's nothing."

"It was worth a shot," Millie said. "Now I want to take a look at Isaac Risang's movements."

Cat exited Brody's file and typed in Isaac's name. "His file is missing."

"Patterson must've pulled it," Annette said.

"That's okay," Millie said. "How about Nevlin Cooper, Brody's cabin mate?" A thought occurred like a bolt of lightning. "Can you go back to the last night in San Juan?"

"No." Cat shook her head. "I think you asked me the other day. I only have information from the last few days; right after the new system was live online."

"Rats. Okay. Let's look at what you have on Nevlin."

Similar to Brody, Nevlin's schedule was consistent. He clocked into work at eleven and clocked out at ten. There was one noticeable difference. Since docking in Miami, Brody hadn't left the dock area and ventured out.

Nevlin, on the other hand, had. Every night, he'd exited the ship via the main gangway around eight p.m. and returned mere minutes before his eleven o'clock shift started.

"That's interesting," Millie murmured. "There's one more. Hugh and I can't remember his last name."

"We looked him up the other day." Cat exited Nevlin's file and typed in Hugh. "I found him. Hugh Mufti. He's a swing shifter."

Annette eased around the counter and stared at the computer. "I must be losing my touch. Why is he on the radar?"

Millie stared at his picture. "He was in the lounge and playing cards the night Isaac was shooting off his mouth."

"I have two separate theories but they could be tied." She shifted her gaze and stared out the window. "What if Nevlin got into a tight situation in the red light district and called on Brody, his friend and cabin mate, to help him out, you know back him up?"

"Ah. Brody shows up at the red light district and other crew from the ship spots him."

"Right. I mean think about it. Brody is a big guy. He wouldn't blend in," Millie said. "Suppose he's trying to protect his friend so he refuses to tell what happened and instead lets people believe he's you-know."

"After Brody is jumped, Nevlin panics, thinking Brody is going to rat him out so he decides to get rid of him," Annette said. "No one knows Brody's schedule better than Nevlin."

"That's one theory, but what if it wasn't Nevlin?" Millie asked. "I think it's something and someone else."

"What about Reef?" Annette asked.

"I thought it was Reef in the beginning, but why would he tear his own office apart and try to break into a locked filing cabinet he more than likely had access to? It doesn't make sense."

"Unless Reef was trying to make it look like someone else," Cat pointed out.

"True, although I'm not sure Reef would think of that." Millie tapped the side of her forehead with her index finger. "Cat, can you track when employees exit and re-enter the employee gangways?"

"Yes." Cat nodded.

"Can I look at Hugh Mufti's log one more time?"

"Sure." Cat turned her attention to the computer screen. "His on board employee charge account balance is huge and thirty days overdue." Cat shifted to the side. "Here's his information."

Millie slipped her reading glasses on, leaned forward and ran her finger along the screen. "This does make it easy to see when employees leave and return."

"Aha! There it is. The proverbial needle in the haystack," Millie said triumphantly. "Patterson told me it's not uncommon for crewmembers to up and quit without giving notice. He also said there were two employees who left the ship when we docked in Miami the other day and they never returned."

Her heart skipped a beat. "Cat, can you tell who those two employees are?"

"Yeah. This program is powerful. I'm sure the two that never returned have been fired."

She squinted her eyes. "Ramos Cruz and Francisco Garcia."

Millie's pulse began to race. "Can you tell me what departments they work in?"

"Ramos worked in housekeeping and Francisco..." Cat's voice trailed off. "Francisco Garcia worked in maintenance."

"I think I'm onto something." Millie lifted her radio. "Danielle, do you copy?"

"Go ahead Millie."

"Can you meet me in Ocean Treasures as soon as possible?"

"I'm on my way."

Millie began to pace as she put the pieces in place.

When Danielle arrived, Millie hurried to the door and motioned her inside. "I think I'm onto something. I need you to look at an employee profile and tell me if you've ever seen this man before."

Millie led Danielle to the computer. "Cat, can you pull up the picture of Francisco Garcia, the man who worked in maintenance?"

"Sure." Cat typed in the computer. "Here's his profile." She stepped to the side and Millie waved Danielle forward. "Do you recognize this man?"

Danielle studied Francisco's image. "Yeah. I haven't seen him in a while but he likes to play poker with some of the other guys down in the lounge."

"With Isaac Risang and Hugh Mufti?"

Danielle's eyes widened. "Yes. There were a few others but those two were regulars." She pointed at the image on the screen. "He was, too. They played with poker chips but I'm pretty sure money exchanged hands, too."

"What if Hugh owed Francisco money? Hugh decided to kill him and dump his body overboard right before we docked. Brody, who was patrolling the corridor, heard the muffled thumps of Francisco's attack."

She continued. "Hugh heard Brody coming so he hid nearby. Brody found Francisco lying on the floor and when he leaned over to check on him, Hugh attacked Brody from behind."

Annette picked up. "After knocking Brody out, Hugh dumped Francisco's body over the side of the ship before we reached port."

"But before he threw him over, Hugh took Francisco's keycard. When the ship docked, he dinged Francisco's keycard to make it look like he left the ship and never returned."

"The security guards who man the exits don't check identification going off the ship, only coming back on," Annette said.

"Later that day, Hugh used *his own* identification to come back on board." Millie tapped her finger on the screen. "Right there. It shows Hugh Mufti returning to the ship but if you look back at his log, you can see that he never left the ship."

"Which means he got off using someone else's keycard," Millie said. "There's one other person who might be able to offer a clue."

"Who?" Cat asked.

"Sharky." Millie turned to Annette. "I need something to bribe him."

"I might have just the ticket. Amit is in the kitchen, working on a deep dish lasagna for dinner."

"That'll work." Millie nodded.

Chapter 21

"You're back again?" Sharky dropped the clipboard on his desk and eyed the dish in Millie's hand. "You must've read my mind. I was just getting ready to run out and grab some grub."

"I need a little favor," Millie said as she lifted the cover on the dish. "I brought a fresh-from-the-oven dish of lasagna and some garlic bread."

Sharky smacked his lips as he eyed the food. "I love lasagna."

"Great. It's all yours just as soon as you answer my question," Millie said.

"What's that?"

"I'll ask it as soon as Dave Patterson arrives."

"Why-" A knock on the door interrupted Sharky's question.

"I'm sure that's him." Millie walked to the door and pulled it open. "Thanks for coming down here." She stepped to the side and Patterson made his way into the office.

"This better be good."

"It will be, at least I hope it will be." Millie pointed at Sharky's cabinet and the bent drawer. "You mentioned earlier that you keep the 'good stuff' inside the filing cabinet and I'm sure that includes employee files and disciplinary reports."

"Yep." Sharky nodded.

"Have you or the night shift supervisor, Reef Savage, ever written up Francisco Garcia and Hugh Mufti?"

Sharky's jaw dropped. He glanced at Patterson, who gave a slight nod. "A couple weeks ago, Reef caught the two of 'em playing cards in here when they shoulda been working. He wrote them up. I guess Francisco got ticked because he walked off the job when we docked in Miami the other day."

"Or maybe he didn't walk off," Millie murmured. She slid the dish of food across the desk. "Thanks Sharky. You've been most helpful."

Patterson and Millie exited Sharky's office. "What was that all about?"

Two maintenance crewmembers passed them in the hall.

"I'll tell you in a minute, but first I'd like to go back to the scene of the crime, I mean one of the crime scenes," Millie said. "Can you show me where Brody was found unconscious the other night?"

"Sure." Patterson led the way and Millie followed him through a maze of corridors and finally into a narrow side corridor. "This is the spot."

Millie studied the floor and then the doors that lined the corridor. "Hugh Mufti, Isaac Risang and Francisco Garcia played poker quite often in the employee lounge. Word has it that money changed hands. I also know Hugh racked up a substantial balance on his employee on board account."

"So?" Patterson prompted.

"I think Hugh owed both Isaac and Francisco money from the poker games. Hugh and Francisco got into it the other night. One thing led to another and Hugh killed Francisco. Brody happened to be in the wrong place at the wrong time and interrupted Hugh during the crime."

She went on to explain her theory that when Brody arrived to investigate some odd noises, he found Francisco lying on the corridor floor. Brody leaned over to check on Francisco and Hugh, who was hiding in one of the storage closets, hit Brody on the back of the head, knocking him out. While Brody was out, Hugh disposed of Francisco's body off the side of the ship but not before taking his employee keycard.

"You told me yourself that two employees left the ship. Francisco Garcia was one of them."

The expression on Patterson's face told her she was on the right track. "If you check the employee log, you'll see that Hugh Mufti returned to the ship the day we docked in Miami but there's no record of him leaving."

Patterson rocked back on his heels. "Because he used another employee's keycard to get off."

"Bingo." Millie nodded. "Francisco Garcia's card."

"You seem to know a great deal about the employee tracking log," Patterson said. "How does Isaac Risang's death tie into all this?"

"Security was called down to the employee lounge the other night because Isaac Risang and a couple others, including Hugh Mufti, were getting rowdy. Brody was the one who showed up and he told them to settle down. After Brody left, I think Hugh egged Isaac into confronting Brody out near the guard gate. What if Hugh heard rumors of Brody's claim he saw someone lying in the corridor, right before he was attacked? Maybe he was worried Brody might remember something and he was desperate to get rid of him. Again, my theory is Hugh owed Isaac money and saw an opportunity to get rid of Isaac and pin it on Brody."

Patterson nodded. "I'll bring Hugh in for questioning, after I view the employee logs myself and question some of the bartenders about the regulars who play poker. If you're right and Mufti clocked back in but never clocked out, we may have something." He paused. "Francisco Garcia left all of his belongings behind when he exited the ship and never returned."

Millie and Patterson headed up the stairs and stopped on the employee crew deck. "Promise me you'll let me know what happens."

"I will, Millie," Patterson said. "I'd still like to know how you accessed the crewmembers' logs."

"I refuse to answer on the grounds I would likely incriminate myself." Millie thanked Patterson for taking her theories seriously before continuing up the stairs.

She was wound tighter than a top and needed something to take her mind off Brody, Isaac and possibly a third victim, Francisco, and she knew exactly how to do that.

Captain Armati and his men were standing outside on the viewing deck. Millie waited until they turned around and she caught the captain's eye.

He said something to Staff Captain Vitale and then made his way inside. "You must have read my mind. I was going to radio you."

Millie's heart skipped a beat. Nic was a sight for sore eyes. It had been a long couple of days, and seemed like an eternity since he'd made her dinner the other night. "It appears you're no worse for the wear since pulling an all-nighter down in maintenance."

The tips of Millie's ears burned. "You heard?"

"Did I ever." The captain rocked back on his heels. "A very angry Sherman, aka Sharky Kiveski, was on my doorstep early this morning, spouting something about a staff member named Missy and another woman from the ship's galley who ransacked his office and bribed him and his night supervisor to let them borrow work uniforms."

"And I was the first person who came to mind?" Millie asked innocently.

"Without a doubt," Nic said. "Andy plans to have a nice long chat with you as soon as he finds you."

"Great." Millie slumped against the wall. "I was off duty."

"But posing as a crewmember."

"Did I break a rule?" Millie asked.

Nic grinned, a twinkle in his eye. "Not that I'm aware of. I can't recall ever having a staff member pose as a night maintenance crewmember. I should take you back to my apartment and punish you severely."

"Promise?" she teased. "If that's the case, I'll be looking for trouble around every corner."

Captain Vitale stepped back into the bridge and Millie glanced around the side of Nic. "Hello Captain Vitale."

"Millie." He gave a small wave. "We heard that you're tearing the ship apart."

Millie groaned and rolled her eyes. "Does everyone know?"

"Not everyone. Mr. Kiveski was in here earlier, ranting and raving like a madman," Vitale said. "You must've done a real number on his office."

"I did not touch his office," Millie insisted. "Other than to clean it up so he wouldn't report me, which he did anyways. Snake."

She changed the subject. "I can't find Andy to get today's schedule, but now that I know I'm in for a lecture I'm not sure I want to find him. Perhaps Scout would like to get some fresh air."

"I'm sure he would love it." The captain led Millie to his apartment and held the door while she stepped inside.

When they were alone, he cornered her in the small hall and pulled Millie into his arms. "Now for your punishment," Nic said as he lowered his head and gently kissed her lips.

Finally, he lifted his head and Millie ran her hand down the side of his face. "I deserved every bit of that."

"And more." He managed to kiss her once more before Scout barreled down the hall and pounced on Millie's shoe.

"There you are." She scooped him up and held him close. "Are you ready to fly the coop?"

Nic pulled Scout's carrier from the hall closet and carried it out of the apartment and to the bridge door. When they reached the exit, Millie hooked his leash to his collar.

"Be sure to keep her out of trouble," Nic told his pooch before shifting his gaze.

"Try to stay out of trouble today, eh?" He didn't wait for a reply as he winked at Millie and slowly closed the bridge door.

Chapter 22

Millie and Scout walked the ship from top to bottom and stem to stern before wandering out onto the dock.

A large crane was in the process of lifting one of the new hot tubs toward the top of the ship.

Millie stood back and watched for several moments. She was awestruck by the size of the tub and offered a simple prayer for the crew's safety.

They wandered to the front of the ship and slowly made their way back. Near the guard gate, Millie spied a strip of green grass, a bench and a shade tree on the other side.

"Shall we?" She placed Scout in his carrier before they slipped out of the gate.

They cleared the dock area and Millie noticed a larger grassy area farther down, so they made their way to the green oasis and she set Scout on a patch of grass.

Scout darted back and forth, as he sniffed the tree, the grass and a small bush. After taking care of business, he trotted over to Millie and settled at her feet. "I'm sorry it's such a small area," she said as she patted his head and gently tugged on the tuft of fur between his ears.

Millie set him on the bench beside her and they watched as the stevedores unloaded the back of a semi-truck. The week had flown by and soon it would be time for Andy to leave the ship.

A bolt of fear inched up her back. What if it wasn't smooth sailing while Andy was on leave? What if she failed miserably and everyone realized she wasn't capable of filling in for her boss and they decided to fire her?

She pushed the thought aside and closed her eyes as a warm breeze tossed her hair. Scout let out a low whine and Millie glanced down. "I bet you're thirsty. Shame on me for not bringing water with us."

Millie tucked Scout inside his carrier, shut the door and they began the short walk back to the ship.

Yellow police tape surrounded the storage area and rock-climbing wall. Millie offered up a small prayer for Isaac and his loved ones.

After stopping by the upper deck to hunt down a small snack and water, they headed to the Sky Chapel on deck fourteen.

The Sky Chapel was one of Millie's favorite spots on board the ship. It was a peaceful oasis in a crazy world, especially when the ship was packed with passengers.

The chapel was cool and quiet and Millie made her way to a bench near the front.

She let Scout out of his carrier to explore the chapel while her mind wandered. Millie gazed at the cross and thought of her upcoming wedding...if there would even be one.

What would Nic and she do if the cruise line told them they could not remain on the same ship if they married? She made a mental note to do a little on line research to see if anyone else had run into the same thing. Surely, they had.

"I thought I heard someone inside the chapel." Pastor Pete Evans wandered to the pew and eased in next to Millie.

Scout trotted over to greet him and the pastor bent down to pat his head. "Hello Sir Scout." The pooch nudged the pastor's hand in greeting and then scampered off. "So what brings you to my neck of the woods?"

"Everything. The usual," Millie said.

"Would one of those be the young crewmember whose body was found near the gate?"

"Yeah. I'm also worried about Brody Rourke. I hope he's not going down for Isaac's death. I'm convinced he's innocent."

Pastor Evans nodded. "I've spoken with Brody at length. He visited me this morning after finishing his night shift. Brody is a loyal friend, perhaps too loyal."

"I agree." Millie sighed heavily. "I'm also worried that Nic, I mean Captain Armati and I won't be able to wed." She glanced at her sparkling diamond engagement ring.

"What if the cruise line refuses to let us marry?" Millie asked in a small voice.

"We pray," the pastor said. "Hard."

"I have been."

"What if we pray together?" Pastor Evans quoted Matthew 18:19. "*Again, truly I tell you that if two of you on earth agree about anything they ask for, it will be done for them by my Father in heaven. Let's pray.*"

Millie bowed her head and closed her eyes.

"Dear Heavenly Father. We come to you today with Millie's heavy heart. Lord, You know her situation, You know her plans to wed Captain Armati and You know what stands in their way.

Your Word says whatever we ask for in prayer and believe we have received it, that it will be ours. We ask you to move Millie's mountain and believe your word that it shall come to pass.

Lord, we also lift up young Isaac and his family, that you stay close to the family and give them peace in this time of mourning. Amen."

"Amen," Millie echoed and lifted her head. "I feel better already."

The pastor stood and Millie followed suit. "I haven't seen you in church the last couple of Sundays."

"Yeah. I've had to work. I'm hoping this week I'll be able to make it." She remembered Andy's imminent departure. "Or maybe not. Andy is taking an emergency leave to take care of his mother and I'm filling in."

"Oh dear," Pastor Pete said. "I should have prayed for all of us."

Millie grinned. "Hey. It's not gonna be that bad."

Scout led the way as they meandered to the church exit. She said good-bye to Pastor Evans and then headed to the sky deck railing.

It was late afternoon and the sun was starting to go down. It was time for her to take Scout home and time to track down Brody.

***

Millie found Brody in the crew dining room. Since most of the crew and staff were taking advantage of eating upstairs, the place was empty except for a few workers behind the buffet area.

"Just the person I was looking for." Millie sat in the chair opposite her friend and watched as he took a big bite of pizza.

"The latest gossip around here is how two old ladies, dressed up in maintenance uniforms, were apprehended near the scene of Isaac's death."

"Someone is embellishing the truth," Millie said. "Annette and I did a great job of keeping an eye on you, huh?"

"Yeah, for me," Brody said. "Not so much for Isaac." He shoved the rest of the piece of pizza in his mouth and chewed loudly.

Millie pointed at the shiner on his chin. "Your bruise is starting to fade."

"I know that Patterson talked to you." She lowered her voice, although there was no one around. "I think that Nevlin, your cabin mate, got into some sort of incident in the red light district last time we stopped in San Juan and you went there to bail him out."

"Nevlin is my friend," Brody said. "He was at a bar, misplaced his cash and asked me to bring him a few bucks to pay his tab. End of story."

"The night shift maintenance crew was giving you a hard time because several of them saw you going inside the *Emerald Isle Club* and I think a killer on board this ship was using that information to his advantage. Do you know who Francisco Garcia is?"

"The name sounds familiar but I don't know him," Brody said.

"What about Hugh Mufti?" Millie asked.

"Yeah. He works in maintenance," Brody said. "I've had to get onto him and Isaac Risang, among others, down in the lounge when they get out of control and obnoxious during their poker playing games."

"Do they play for money?" Millie asked.

"They're not supposed to but I'm pretty sure they do."

Millie leaned back in her chair. "Isaac Risang is dead and Francisco Garcia, another one of the regulars at the poker table, left the ship. What if

Francisco didn't leave the ship? What if he was the person you found lying on the ground the other night?"

"Why him?" Brody asked.

"My theory is Hugh got into an argument with Francisco over money. It turned violent and Hugh killed him. Hugh was worried you saw something and he was desperate to get rid of you. Isaac Risang either knew something or Hugh Mufti owed him money so Hugh wanted to silence him, too, and found the perfect opportunity by setting you up."

Millie shifted in her seat. "The whole harassment by other night maintenance crew was just a cover up, a non-issue. If my theories are correct, Dave Patterson will soon arrest a killer, Hugh Mufti."

Brody crumpled his napkin and tossed it on top of his empty plate. "I have no idea how you figure this stuff out but I think you missed your calling in life."

Millie hopped out of her chair and circled the table. "No. I think I'm doing exactly what I should be doing." She gave him a quick hug. "Saving my friends from themselves."

Chapter 23

"What do you think?" Millie twisted to the side so Cat, Annette and Danielle had a clear view of the elegant V-neck fitted dress. The cap sleeve wedding dress was the perfect length and it brushed the bottom of Millie's knees. A decorative beaded band circled her waist.

"Turn around." Cat made a twirling motion with her finger.

Millie slowly twirled.

"Is it comfortable?" Annette asked. "Can you sit without splitting a seam?"

"I hadn't thought of that." Millie glided to an overstuffed ottoman and perched on the edge. "Yes. It's kinda stretchy."

"Perfect." Danielle gave two thumbs up. "You look like a million bucks. What about the veil?"

"No veil." Millie shook her head. "I plan to have my hair up with some loose ringlets on each side. I'm going for a chic upsweep."

The sales clerk appeared. "It's a beautiful dress. What do you think?"

"I'll take it," Millie said. "I'll need three bridesmaid dresses for my attendees."

"What?" Cat shrieked. "You want us to stand up with you?"

"I don't do dresses," Danielle said.

"Me either," Annette chimed in.

"Come on," Millie begged. "Not even for my special day?"

Danielle groaned.

Annette wagged her finger at Millie. "The things we do for you."

"That's what I thought." Millie turned to the clerk. "I'll be purchasing my dress plus their three. Let me take this off so we can start looking for them."

"What about pantsuits?" Annette asked.

"When's the last time you wore a dress?" Millie asked.

Annette thought for a moment. "High school."

"Annette," Cat chuckled. "Humor Millie. No one will see you but us two. You, too." She pointed at Danielle.

The women finally relented. Millie and Cat had fun dressing their friends in several foo foo dresses before they settled on elegant, yet casual, tea length dresses in a spectacular shade of gray aptly named mist.

The dresses were ones the women could wear more than once and after the clerk bagged all four, Millie paid for them with her charge card.

They exited the store, each carrying their garment.

"Now for lunch," Millie said. "I found an off-the-beaten-path Bayfront seafood restaurant not far from here. We'll have to take a taxi."

Taxis lined the streets of the shopping district. The women grabbed the nearest one, careful not to wrinkle their dresses as they crammed inside the back seat while Millie slid into the front passenger seat.

When they reached the restaurant, the hostess seated them at a table overlooking the bay. After they placed their orders, Annette turned to Millie. "I heard Patterson turned Hugh Mufti over to the local authorities."

"Yeah. Patterson checked the video surveillance near the gangway exit at the time Francisco supposedly exited the ship and the person using the card was not Francisco." Millie sipped her water and set the glass down.

"It was Hugh Mufti," Cat said. "So the whole Brody and the gay bar angle was just a cover?"

"Yep," Millie said. "Brody just happened to be in the wrong place at the wrong time."

"There's one other serious matter we haven't touched on." Millie turned to Danielle. "Have you heard anything from Patterson on the investigation into the date drug?"

"Date drug?" Cat gasped.

Danielle explained the incident in the crew bar, how she suspected someone had slipped something into her drink. "Unfortunately, I don't have proof and I can't remember what the guys at the bar looked like."

She went on. "So far, I'm the only one who reported that type of incident so I think they're going to wait to see if it's isolated."

"Don't go to the bar alone," Millie warned.

"Trust me, I'll be careful. If I have to use the bathroom, I'll dump the drink out when I return and order another one," Danielle promised.

The conversation drifted to Cat and Doctor Gundervan's relationship. Cat was vague, telling her friends they were trying to take it slow.

"How was your date the other day?" Millie asked. "Did you have a good time?"

"The shopping part was fun." Cat sipped her water. "We were going to stop by South Beach so we could say we've been there but once we caught a glimpse of the beachgoers and some skimpy beach attire, we changed our minds."

When they finished eating, the girls gathered their things and caught a taxi back to the ship. It had been a wonderful day and a welcome break from the frantic pace of life on board the ship.

After dinging their key cards, Alison, one of the dancers, stopped them before they reached the stairs. "You have to sign the petition before you can go downstairs."

"Petition?" Millie glanced at the clipboard Alison was holding.

"Yes. We've started a petition to send to Majestic Cruise Lines in support of someone's upcoming nuptials."

"You're kidding." Millie looked at Alison and then the clipboard. It was full of signatures, asking the cruise line to allow Captain Armati and Millie to remain on board and together. There was page after page of signatures and sudden tears burned her eyes. "You did this for me?" she whispered.

"Of course silly." Alison handed Millie the pen. "We're not letting you go anywhere. This place would be as dull as a butter knife."

Millie signed her name with flourish and handed the pen to Cat, who was standing next to her.

"We have over 900 signatures already," Alison said.

Annette was the last to sign. She handed the pen and clipboard to Alison. "Alison is right. Life wouldn't be the same without you Millie."

"I can't wait to see what happens next week while Andy is gone," Alison joked.

Millie frowned. "Thanks for reminding me. Neither can I, Alison. Neither can I."

The end.

If you enjoyed reading "Cruisin' for a Bruisin'," please take a moment to leave a review. It would be greatly appreciated! Thank you!

The Series Continues...Look for Book 10 in the "Cruise Ship Cozy Mysteries" Series Coming Soon!

List of Books by Hope Callaghan

Made in Savannah Cozy Mystery Series

Key to Savannah: Book 1
Road to Savannah: Book 2
Justice in Savannah: Book 3
Swag in Savannah: Book 4
Trouble in Savannah: Book 5
Book 6: Coming Soon!

Garden Girls Cozy Mystery Series

Who Murdered Mr. Malone? Book 1
Grandkids Gone Wild: Book 2
Smoky Mountain Mystery: Book 3
Death by Dumplings: Book 4
Eye Spy: Book 5
Magnolia Mansion Mysteries: Book 6
Missing Milt: Book 7
Bully in the 'Burbs: Book 8
Fall Girl: Book 9
Home for the Holidays: Book 10
Sun, Sand, and Suspects: Book 11
Look Into My Ice: Book 12
Forget Me Knot: Book 13
Nightmare in Nantucket: Book 14
Greed with Envy: Book 15
Book 16: Coming Soon!
Garden Girls Box Set I – (Books 1-3)
Garden Girls Box Set II – (Books 4-6)

Cruise Ship Cozy Mystery Series

Starboard Secrets: Book 1
Portside Peril: Book 2
Lethal Lobster: Book 3
Deadly Deception: Book 4
Vanishing Vacationers: Book 5
Cruise Control: Book 6
Killer Karaoke: Book 7
Suite Revenge: Book 8
Cruisin' for a Bruisin': Book 9
Book 10: Coming Soon!
Cruise Ship Cozy Mysteries Box Set I (Books 1-3)
Cruise Ship Cozy Mysteries Box Set II (Books 4-6)

Sweet Southern Sleuths Cozy Mysteries Short Stories Series

Teepees and Trailer Parks: Book 1
Bag of Bones: Book 2
Southern Stalker: Book 3
Two Settle the Score: Book 4
Killer Road Trip: Book 5
Pups in Peril: Book 6
Dying To Get Married-In: Book 7
Deadly Drive-In: Book 8
Secrets of a Stranger: Book 9

Library Lockdown: Book 10
Vandals & Vigilantes: Book 11
Fatal Frolic: Book 12
Sweet Southern Sleuths Box Set I: (Books 1-4)
Sweet Southern Sleuths Box Set: II: (Books 5-8)
Sweet Southern Sleuths Box Set III: (Books 9-12)
Sweet Southern Sleuths 12 Book Box Set (Entire Series)

Samantha Rite Deception Mystery Series

Waves of Deception: Book 1
Winds of Deception: Book 2
Tides of Deception: Book 3
Samantha Rite Series Box Set – (Books 1-3-The Complete Series)

Get Free Books and More!

Sign up for my Free Cozy Mysteries Newsletter to get free and discounted books, giveaways & soon-to-be-released books!

hopecallaghan.com/newsletter

Meet The Author

Hope Callaghan is an author who loves to write Christian books, especially Christian Mystery and Cozy Mystery books. She has written more than 50 mystery books (and counting) in five series.

In March 2017, Hope won a Mom's Choice Award for her book, "Key to Savannah," Book 1 in the Made in Savannah Cozy Mystery Series.

Born and raised in a small town in West Michigan, she now lives in Florida with her husband.

She is the proud mother of one daughter and a stepdaughter and stepson. When she's not doing the thing she loves best - writing books - she enjoys cooking, traveling and reading books.

Hope loves to connect with her readers! Connect with her today!

Visit **hopecallaghan.com** for special offers, free books, and soon-to-be-released books!

Email: hope@hopecallaghan.com

Facebook:
https://www.facebook.com/hopecallaghanauthor/

Annette's Super Easy Ooey Gooey Chocolate Melting Cake Recipe

Ingredients:

¾ cup (6 oz.) dark chocolate chips (I used Nestle's 53% cacao chips)
¾ cup (6 oz.) butter
4 eggs – room temperature
¾ cup (6 oz.) white sugar
1/8 tablespoon vanilla extract
¼ cup (2 oz.) all-purpose flour
Powdered sugar*

*Use 8 oz. ramekin baking dishes. Makes 4 servings.

Directions:

Preheat oven to 375 degrees.
Melt chocolate and butter in small saucepan.
Cool 10 minutes.
While chocolate and butter is cooling, whisk eggs, sugar and vanilla in medium size bowl.
Add flour to eggs/sugar mixture. Mix thoroughly.

Mix chocolate with other ingredients.
Fill ramekin dishes ¾ of the way full with chocolate batter.
Bake for 14 minutes. Do not overcook. Outsides should be firm (cakelike) and middle should be gooey.
Remove. Cool for a couple moments and serve with vanilla ice cream.

*Optional: sprinkle top with powdered sugar after baking.

Made in the USA
Columbia, SC
05 March 2021